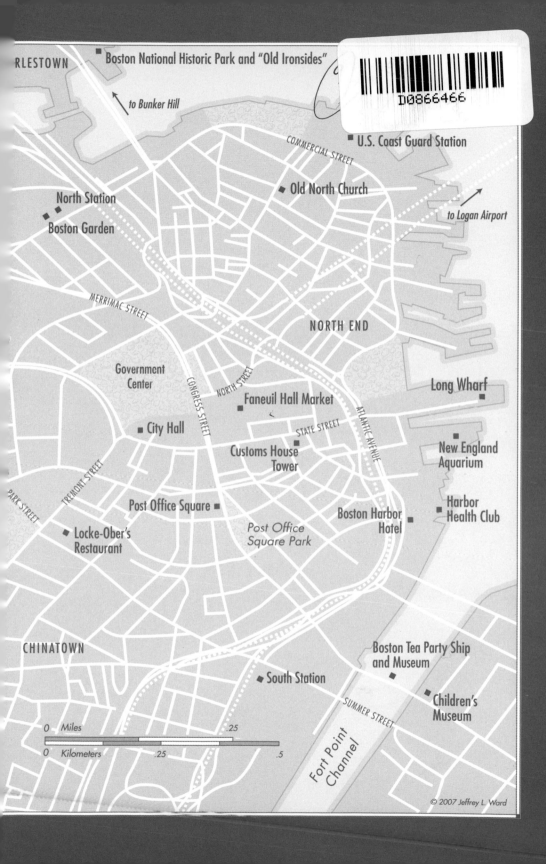

RLESTOWN

Boston National Historic Park and "Old Ironsides"

to Bunker Hill

COMMERCIAL STREET

U.S. Coast Guard Station

Old North Church

to Logan Airport

North Station

Boston Garden

MERRIMAC STREET

NORTH END

Long Wharf

Government Center

CONGRESS STREET

NORTH STREET

Faneuil Hall Market

STATE STREET

ATLANTIC AVENUE

New England Aquarium

City Hall

Customs House Tower

TREMONT STREET

Post Office Square

PARK STREET

Post Office Square Park

Boston Harbor Hotel

Harbor Health Club

Locke-Ober's Restaurant

CHINATOWN

Boston Tea Party Ship and Museum

South Station

Children's Museum

SUMMER STREET

Fort Point Channel

0 Miles   .25
0 Kilometers   .25   .5

© 2007 Jeffrey L. Ward

SLOW BURN

THE SPENSER NOVELS

ROBERT B. PARKER'S
SLOW BURN

ACE ATKINS

G. P. PUTNAM'S SONS
NEW YORK

G. P. PUTNAM'S SONS
Publishers Since 1838
An imprint of Penguin Random House LLC
375 Hudson Street
New York, New York 10014

ISBN 9780399170850

Printed in the United States of America
1   3   5   7   9   10   8   6   4   2

BOOK DESIGN BY MEIGHAN CAVANAUGH

In memory of Elvis,

a true wonder dog

SLOW BURN

K evin always loved fire. His earliest memories were of his mother taking him to blazes, watching men in helmets and heavy coats pull hoses into burning buildings. He loved the way she looked at those men with honor and respect, and maybe something more. Just the crackle of the scanner, a far-off bell ringing, smoke trailing up into the sky made his heart jackhammer. When he drove through the night in his old Crown Vic, he felt like he owned the freakin' city.

He kept the scanner under the dashboard, a big antenna set on the trunk as he roamed the streets of Hyde Park, Roxbury, Dorchester, Jamaica Plain, Brookline, and up into Cambridge and Charlestown. All that spring and summer, Kevin liked to drive slow, windows down, listening, waiting, and sniffing the air. He'd work his deadbeat job during the day, sleeping through most of it, and then take on the city at night. He, Johnny, and Big Ray would meet up at Scandinavian Pastry in Southie, taking breaks off patrol to talk call boxes, famous fires, new equipment, and all the ways the current administration was fucking up a long, proud tradition.

"Cocoanut Grove," Johnny said, powdered sugar on his mustache. "It could happen again. Payoffs, bribes, and all these damn foreigners in this town. You just wait. Some asshole's gonna be changing a lightbulb and poof."

"Nobody gives a crap," Ray said. "I've been warning the fire guys for ten years. Their equipment has turned to shit. They just don't get it. Mayor won't approve the new budget. Not with a gun to his nuts."

And he'd look up at them, in that little corner Formica-topped table and ask, why don't they do something? Why don't they take action and save this city?

Kevin thought about this long and hard. He and Johnny had talked about it a thousand times. And he'd finally agreed to Johnny's master plan. Save the tradition. Keep Boston safe. Knock people in the side of the head and make 'em listen. The city needed firefighters—and a lot more of them. Guys ready to serve who were shut out. He met Johnny's eyes across the table. Johnny nodded and said, "Burn it."

"Burn what?" Ray said. "Hey, you gonna eat that maple glazed? I've only had two."

Kevin didn't say anything, just leaned back farther in the booth, arm stretched out wide behind Johnny. Short, *squat Johnny cutting his eyes over at him and lifting an eyebrow. The scanner clucking off and on. Some bullshit Dumpster fire over by the T on Dot Ave. Probably a couple bums roasting a hot dog.*

"We understand what's wrong with the department," Johnny said, wiping the sugar off his face. "It's the only way. We got the know-how and the skills to make it work."

Big Ray looked to each of them with wide, nutty eyes, waiting for someone to tell him what the hell was going on. The scanner caught again, sending the ladder truck and EMS back to the station. False alarm. Silence. Nothing. Fluorescent lights burning over the donut displays, cash register empty, unmanned. No one minding the store at two a.m.

"Burn it," he said. "Johnny is right."

"Burn what?" Big Ray said. "What the hell?"

"Boston, you fucking moron," Johnny said. "We burn fucking Boston."

1

The Harbor Health Club had returned to its roots.

Not only was boxing allowed, it was now encouraged by Henry Cimoli. For a waterfront gym that had weathered both urban renewal and Zumba, the time had come. Henry and I took a break from the boxing ring and watched a dozen or so young professionals, men and women, listen to a Cree Indian from Montana teach them how to deliver a left jab.

Henry had a welded cage built in the expanse of what had been the workout room, heavy bags swinging from the platform. Half the gym was now boxing, the other half free weights and CrossFit gear. Hawk and I were quite pleased. Not to mention Z, whom Henry had employed for the last two years and who had ushered in the new era.

"You didn't have to do all of this for us."

"I did it for Mr. Green," he said, rubbing his thumb and two fingers together. "What makes the world go 'round."

"What if aerobics come back in style?"

"I'll bring in fucking monkeys on unicycles if it'll keep this gym open," he said. "If you hadn't noticed, this building isn't on skid row anymore."

"I could tell by the yachts moored outside," I said. "I pick up on subtle clues like that."

We leaned against the ropes, like cowboys on a split-rail fence, watching Z help a fit young woman in a pink sports bra throw a left hook.

"To be young," Henry said.

"'The moments passed as at a play,'" I said.

"And I have the ex-wives to prove it," Henry said, letting himself out of the ropes and down the short steps. He walked over to help Z instruct the lithe young woman. I admired his commitment.

I spent a half-hour on a treadmill, showered, and changed into my street clothes: Levi's, black pocket T-shirt, and a pair of tan suede desert boots. As I was headed to the street, a rotund man in a gray sweatshirt whistled for me. He'd been running the dumbbell rack with biceps curls, his fat face flushed and sweaty.

Jack McGee wiped a towel over his neck and said, "Christ, Spenser. I been waiting for you all freakin' morning."

"Nice to be needed."

I shook his wet hand. Jack sweated a lot. He was a short, thick guy with Irish written all over his face. I'd known him for many years, and in the many I'd known him he'd been a Boston firefighter. Being a firefighter was more than a job for Jack, it was a calling.

"I got a problem," he said. Whispering, although most of Henry's clients were in the boxing room.

"Superset your bis and tris," I said. "Work the dumbbells with press-downs."

"Are you busy with anything right now?"

I shrugged. "I just finished an insurance-fraud case," I said. "But I'm always on standby for the big *S* projected into the clouds over Boston."

"Well, I got a big fucking *S* for you," he said. "As in the shit has hit the fan."

"I'm familiar with that *S*."

"There's this thing."

"There's always a thing," I said.

"Can we talk outside?"

McGee followed me out to my newish blue Explorer. I tossed my gym bag into the back and leaned against the door with my arms folded over my chest. I had worked out hard and my biceps bulged from my T-shirt. I feared if I stood there any longer, I might be accosted by passing women.

"You know about the fire last year?" McGee said.

Everyone knew about the fire last year. Three firefighters had died at an old church in the South End. The funeral Mass had been televised on local TV. There had been an inquiry. I'd never spoken to Jack about it other than to offer my condolences.

"For the last year, I've been saying it was arson," he said. "But no one's been arrested and I hear things have stalled out. It's always tomorrow with those guys. And now we're getting shit burning nearly every night. This city's got an arsonist loose and no one wants to admit it."

"You think it's connected to the church?"

"Damn right," he said. "But no one is saying shit in the department. I lost my best friend, Pat Dougherty, in that church. We went through the academy together. Then at Engine 33/ Ladder 15 for the first three years. Godfather to his kids. Same neighborhood. Jesus, you know."

I nodded again. I told him I was very sorry.

"Mike Mulligan hadn't been on the job but six months," McGee said. "A rake. An open-up man. His dad was a fireman. He was a Marine like me. Saw some shit over in Afghanistan only to come home and get killed."

I opened up the driver's door and let the windows down. It was June and the morning had grown warm. No one was complaining. We'd just survived the longest, snowiest winter since Grant was president. "Why do you think the church is connected to the new fires?"

"Call it firemen's intuition."

"Got anything more than that?" I said.

"That church wasn't an accident," he said. "Everybody knows it. Arson sifted through that shit pile for months. No signs of electrical or accidental. It's a fucking fire of unknown origin. How's that sit with Pat's wife and kids?"

"Arson investigation is a pretty specialized field," I said. "Most of the clues burn up."

"I don't need more samples and microscopes," he said. "I'll pay you 'cause you know the worst people in the city. Some scum who'd do something like this. Burn a fucking Catholic church and then keep burning through Southie and the South End until they're caught."

"Over the years, I've met a few people of questionable breeding."

"Freakin' criminals," Jack said. "I want you to shake the bushes for criminals and find out who set this and why."

"Follow the money?"

"What else could it be?"

I leaned my forearms against my open door. My caseload had waned over the months while my checking account had fattened. Corporations paid more than people. I had few reasons to spurn the offer. Not to mention Jack McGee was an honorable man who'd asked for help.

"Okay," I said. "Will you introduce me around?"

"Nope."

I waited.

"You start making noise at headquarters and the commissioner will have my ass," he said. "All I need is for the commissioner and the chief to get pissed while I'm doing my last few years. I made captain. Got a pension. I got a great firehouse in the North End. I don't want to make waves. I just want some answers."

"No official inquiries?" I said.

"Nope."

"No pressure on arson investigators?"

"Nope," Jack said. "You're going to have to go around your ass to get to your elbow on this one."

"Yikes," I said. "That sounds painful."

"But can you do it?"

"Sure," I said. "I've taken that route many times before."

T o what do I owe this honor?" Quirk said. "Did you just shoot some poor bastard while cleaning your revolver?"

"I just stopped by to admire your new office," I said. "Check out your breathtaking view. Congratulate you on your promotion."

"Bullshit."

"Deputy Superintendent Quirk has a nice ring to it."

"It's ceremonial," Quirk said. "I meet with neighborhood groups. Do press briefings and photo ops."

I saluted him. "Does this mean I can finally meet McGruff the Crime Dog?"

"Yeah," he said. "I'll tell him to hump your leg. After this long on the job, a little boost is appreciated. Might finally be able to retire. Move down to Florida. Get a boat."

"Not in your nature."

"Neither was this," he said. "But it's what I got."

"And Belson?"

"Training the new captain in investigative techniques."

"God help her."

"Amen," Quirk said, leaning in to his desk. His hands were as thick and strong as a bricklayer's. His salt-and-pepper hair looked to have been trimmed that morning. White dress shirt double-starched. Red tie affixed with a gold clip. I knew his wingtips were polished so bright they'd blind me. "So what the hell do you want?"

"There was a fire last year," I said. "A nine-alarm in the South End at the Holy Innocents Catholic Church."

"Yeah, I know."

"You worked the deaths?"

"Of course I did," Quirk said. "You might recall I once ran Homicide. We investigate all fatal fires. You know that."

"And what did you learn?"

"Jack and shit," he said, picking up the square plastic picture frame on his desk. He turned it around in his big hands to study his wife, kids, and numerous grandchildren. He waited a few beats and then leveled his gaze at me. If it was at all possible, his face had hardened in the years I'd known him. Not flesh and bone. More like carved granite. "Whattya know?"

"I'd like to see the interviews."

"It was a fire," he said. "Go talk to fucking Fire."

"I would," I said. "But it's an open investigation. I hoped Boston police might have many of the same files."

"Yeah, well," Quick said. "We just might."

"You do."

"As you said, it's an open investigation, hotshot."

I smiled and shrugged. Quirk frowned.

"You working with a jake?" he said.

"Perhaps."

"A jake who doesn't want people to know he's working with the nosiest snoop in the Back Bay."

"I prefer the most winning profile."

"If I had a nose like that, I wouldn't be one to brag."

"Character," I said. "Built of character."

"And plenty of cotton shoved up your schnoz," Quirk said. He put down the plastic square and pushed back from his desk. He folded his big hands over his chest. "Arson isn't too keen on a guy like you butting into their business."

"I will tread lightly."

"You?" he said. "Yeah, sure. How's Susan?"

"Charming and gorgeous as ever."

"Pearl?"

"Getting old," I said. "Graying around the muzzle. But wiser, like us all."

"I like Susan," he said. "She gives you class."

"I do not disagree."

"Never understood what she sees in you."

"Would you like me to demonstrate a one-arm push-up?"

Quirk held his gaze for a while. He then nodded. "I can't promise anything. But I can make some calls. Ask around."

I nodded back. But I did not move from the chair. It was new and very comfortable.

"Or do you expect for me to leave the heights of my office

and go down and fetch the reports in records like a Labrador retriever?"

"I can wait," I said. "You now have a secretary. Perhaps she might share a little coffee?"

"My *she* is a *he*," Quirk said. "And he makes terrible coffee."

"Coming from you, that's a compliment," I said.

"So your client thinks it was arson."

"Yep."

"Officially, I'll tell you I never heard that," Quirk said. "Unofficially, I'll tell you we took pictures, asked questions, and stepped away. Looked to be accidental. Did I tell you it was my freakin' church when I was a kid?"

"No, you did not."

"Jesus Christ," Quirk said. "Okay. Okay. You got that look in your eye."

"Sanguine?"

"Like you're going to pain my ass until I say okay," he said. "Give me a call in the morning, Spenser. For Christ's sake."

I stood and walked to Quirk's closed door. It was a nice door, but I missed the old one with the frosted glass over on Berkeley. I opened it wide and waited.

"And, Spenser?"

I turned.

"Your favor meter ran out a long while back," he said.

I mimed turning a meter backward and winked at him. Quirk did not smile.

I took Susan and Mattie Sullivan to Fenway that night. Mattie and I ate at the ballpark while Susan held out for postgame at Eastern Standard. Once seated, she promptly ordered a cocktail called The Thaw made with gin, St.-Germain, lime, Peychaud's Bitters, and parsley. I simply nodded toward the Harpoon IPA on tap.

"We should've given Mattie a ride home," Susan said.

"I offered," I said. "She still prefers the T."

"Because she doesn't want to rely on anyone."

"Not a bad trait," I said. "She's known no other way."

Eastern Standard was at the bottom of the Hotel Commonwealth, outfitted with brass, swirling ceiling fans, and red leather booths. The place made me feel as if I were eating inside a Paris train station, with a menu to match. Steaks, frites, oysters.

Since I'd eaten at the game, I kept it to two dozen oysters. Susan had the bluefish with hominy, cherry tomatoes, and romesco sauce. She told me I could pick from her plate.

"Do you remember my pal Jack McGee?" I said.

She shook her head, sipping her cocktail.

"The firefighter?" I said. "He's captain over the house in the North End. We stopped by the house during Saint Anthony's last year."

"I had to pee."

"The firefighters were most gracious."

"Big guy?" she said.

"Some might call Jack somewhat husky," I said. "But he can shimmy up a ladder like nobody's business."

"Sure," Susan said. "Okay."

"Jack's a long-timer at Henry's," I said. "He lost three guys in that church fire in the South End."

Susan nodded. She tilted her head to listen with more intent and complete focus. All the noise around us went silent when she looked at me that way.

"Jack thinks it's arson," I said. "Although, as of yet, there is no official cause."

"And Jack wants you to snoop?"

"I would prefer the term *professionally detect*."

Susan shrugged and took another sip of her cocktail. "And what do you know about arson investigation?"

"About as much as I do about women," I said. "But Jack says most of the evidence burned up in the fire anyway. He wants me to use my contacts with the flotsam and jetsam of Boston."

"He believes the fire to be the work of criminals?"

I nodded.

"But who would burn a church for money?"

"You really want to ask that?" I said.

"I withdraw the question."

"I just hope I can help."

"So you agreed to take the case?"

"He caught me at a good time," I said. "'Summertime and the living is easy.' If I can't get anywhere, I won't charge him."

"Just how much did you charge Mattie Sullivan to find out who killed her mother?"

I grinned and looked down at my knuckles. "Box of donuts."

Susan smiled back. She'd worn a green safari shirt dress, gold hoop earrings, a thin gold chain, and brown gladiator sandals to the game. The outfit really snapped with the Sox cap I'd bought for her at Yawkey Way.

"You know Mattie graduates next year," she said.

I nodded.

"And I understand Z is moving back to Los Angeles?"

I nodded again.

"Does that make us empty-nesters?" she said.

"Have you forgotten Pearl?"

"How could I ever forget the baby," Susan said. "But we both must admit she's getting a bit long in the tooth."

"You know my answer to that."

"We'll just find a new Pearl?"

I sipped some beer. I didn't like to think about it. Outside the window, the stadium continued to empty, with people walking along Comm Ave or down into Kenmore Station. The Sox had lost, but the lights burned bright across the city.

"And what if something happens to you?" Susan said. She grinned with her white, perfect teeth in a devilish way. She tilted back her drink.

"You can have me mounted and stuffed," I said. "Just like Roy did for Dale."

"Roy stuffed Trigger," she said. "Not Dale."

"Similar sentiment."

"Maybe I'll just find a younger man," Susan said. "Someone with less miles on him."

"But could he sing 'Moody's Mood for Love' in Spanish?"

"Can you?"

I took a sip of beer and took a deep breath, just as the oysters and Susan's bluefish arrived.

"Timing is everything," she said.

•

Bright and early the next morning, I drove into the South End to meet with Captain Troy Collins of Engine Company 22. The firehouse was a squat building of little character situated between several churches and office buildings on Tremont. Collins invited me upstairs to the firefighters' quarters and kitchen, where he made some coffee. "McGee warned me you'd be stopping by," he said. "He didn't want to get me in trouble. Told me to keep it on the down low."

"What'd you say?"

"This was Pat D's firehouse," he said. "I'll tell you my deepest, darkest secrets if you think it might help. Him and Mike were like brothers."

Collins was a trim black man in his early fifties with closely cropped gray hair and a short gray mustache. He had a thick chest and muscular arms and walked with the ramrod posture of former military. Two firefighters were in a break room, lying on an old couch and watching CNN; three others were in a back room, lifting weights. I passed a locker with a bumper sticker that read DIAL 911 CUZ SHIT HAPPENS.

"Accurate," I said.

"Saw one the other day that read GOD CREATED FIREMEN SO POLICE COULD HAVE HEROES, TOO."

"I bet cops love that."

"Cops think that Jack, Queen, King is as high as we can count," he said. "Screw 'em. Would you like some cream or sugar?"

I took a teaspoon of sugar. "You guys were the first to arrive?"

"Yeah," he said. "I was off. Dougherty was in charge."

I'd spent my waking hours reading up on Lieutenant Pat Dougherty, Jimmy Bonnelli, and Mike Mulligan from *The Globe*'s online archives. Mulligan was only twenty-four, just back from a second tour of Afghanistan. Bonnelli had nine years on the job, two ex-wives, and three kids. Dougherty was the old-timer, a lifelong friend to Jack McGee. Father to four, a practical joker, a fine cook, and a dedicated Pats fan. He spent most of his years with Engine 33/Ladder 15, the old Back Bay firehouse built in the 1880s.

"It had been a busy night and the boys were eating late," Collins said. "We had some extra in the dinner fund and Dougherty sprung for some nice filets. Wrapped in bacon. He knew a guy who knew a guy in the meat business."

"And right before they sat down—"

"They were in the middle of saying Grace and the alarm goes nuts."

"Always that way?"

"Always," Collins said. "Good food tempts fate."

"How long do you think the fire had been burning?"

"It's not a half-mile from the station," Collins said. He sat down and placed two coffees between us. "Didn't take them a minute to get there. Mike was a great driver. But I heard that church was lit up. Fire eating through plywood and shattering the big stained-glass window. Dougherty struck a second alarm right away."

"I read they went immediately toward the basement?"

"Pat would've seen the fire and smoke down there," he said. "We later found out that's where the church kept their old files, which burned quick and hot. He knew he'd lost the building but wanted to make sure it didn't spread. There's a big new condo a block away, hundreds of people. When they got there some homeless guy was screaming he'd seen someone inside."

"How many went in?"

"All four," he said. "Dougherty and Mulligan led with the hose. Bonnelli and John Grady followed after hooking up to the hydrant."

"You know what happened to the homeless guy?" I said.

"Nope," he said. "There's a methadone clinic around the corner. Neighborhood is in transition, homeless guy could be one of hundreds. I can't tell you much else."

"What about John Grady?"

"He got lucky," Collins said. "Another few feet and he'd have been dead, too."

"I know you weren't there," I said. "But how do you think they got trapped?"

"No secret," he said. He rubbed his short, gray mustache and had a vacant, faraway look in his eyes. "The fucking fire flashed back and blocked the exit. I know the smoke was thick down there. They'd have had to try and braille their way out. You know? On their hands and knees, feeling walls when they died. Like I said, this thing happened quick. It burned hot. All in all, five minutes? I think about those men when I go to sleep and first thing when I wake."

"Do you think it might've been set?"

"No evidence of it," he said. "To be honest, there wasn't a hell of a lot left in that pit."

"But it's possible?"

"Of course." Collins watched me and took a long, deep breath. "Anything's possible. I found it strange how fast the fire burned. And how the fire met in the middle."

"Multiple points of origin?"

"Say, you're pretty smart for a former cop."

I shrugged. "Some of my best friends are firefighters."

Collins grinned and drank some coffee. He made a bitter face and reached for some artificial sweetener.

"The investigation is still open?" I said.

"Unknown origin," he said. "I guess technically it'll always be open."

"Why do you think the fire was set in two locations?"

"Hold on," Collins said. He lifted up his right hand. "Hold on. I never said 'set.' I said it could have *originated* in two places. And I only say that because Mulligan radioed in that two fires were burning at opposite ends of the church before the flashback."

"That didn't register with investigators?"

"Evidence didn't show two sites," Collins said. "And Mike's dead. We can't ask him what he saw."

He gave a weak smile and sipped his coffee.

"I'm very sorry."

"One minute you're laughing and telling jokes and the next thing you know you're riding that red truck into the depths of hell," Collins said. "I miss those fellas every damn day. Like I said, they were brothers. If you hadn't noticed, not many folks who look like me in the ranks."

"Irish?"

"My great-great-grandfather must have been Irish," he said, laughing. "A slave owner down in Georgia."

"I knew it," I said. "You have that twinkle in your eye."

"I wish I knew more," he said. "And I wish I'd been there with them. We got the dedication coming up. They're going to unveil a plaque here at the house. It's pretty much all I can think about. Media and all that stopping by. Folks bringing us more food than we can ever eat."

"I'd like to speak to John Grady."

"That might be tricky," he said.

"He's no longer with your company?"

"Nope." Collins shook his head. "He's on disability. Cracked a couple vertebrae that night. Off the record, I hear he's been drinking a lot. He just never came back from it, physically or mentally."

I asked where I might find him, and he gave me the name of a well-known bar in Dorchester. I nodded and offered my hand. Collins shook it and looked me in the eye.

"What do you think about this church being connected to these latest arsons?"

"Hard to say," Collins said. "We haven't had much rest since spring. Someone or several folks are burning up lots of old buildings. Dumpsters, trash piles. It's keeping us on high alert."

"Jack believes it's all the same."

"I'm not sure about that," Collins said. "Seems to be a different kind of animal at work. Besides, you do know Jack McGee is crazy?"

"Sure," I said. "Why do you think we're friends?"

The Eire Pub was known as Boston's Original Gentlemen's Prestige Bar. Just to underscore the point, it was announced from a rooftop billboard on Adams, across from the Greenhills Irish Bakery and down the street from a run-down funeral home. Staying true to my heritage, I ordered a Guinness. The head was poured so thick and professionally, I could have used it to shave.

The Sox played on flat screens spaced about every two feet. After I sampled the beer, I ordered a corned-beef sandwich and watched another inning. Four potential barflies surrounded me at the largish bar. The walls were decorated with a lot of historic Boston photos. Several had been shot by my friend Bill Brett from *The Globe*. The middle of the bar was divided by an island of whiskey. Through the colorful bottles, I spotted a guy in his early to mid-forties with a lot of brown hair, sipping on a draft.

Two of the other men were too old. A guy seated three stools down wore a collared shirt and had soft hands.

I moved to the other side of the bar and found a stool next to the big guy.

"These fucking bums are killing me," the man said.

"That's what the beer is for."

"It's like last season was some kind of dream."

"You wouldn't happen to be John Grady?"

"Depends on who's asking," he said. "You work for my ex-wife or the fucking insurance company?"

"I work for myself," I said. "I'm a friend of Jack McGee's."

"*Pfft.* Jack McGee," he said. "You know he's a genuine nutso?"

"That seems to be the consensus."

"No, really," he said. "I'm not kidding. He's always been crazy. But lately. Holy Christ. He's got these theories. He won't let this fire go. Can't quit running his mouth. Somehow his brains have gotten all scrambled. Can't believe he made fucking captain."

"He lost a close friend."

"What about me?" Grady said. "I lost three great friends and broke my freaking back. You don't see me blaming bogeymen. Shit happens, you know? You think there's order in this universe, but no one is driving the fucking bus."

"Baseball, beer, and existentialism," I said.

"You trying to get smart?"

"Too early in the day." I sipped the second half of my Guinness. Ortiz hit a ball far and a little too high.

Grady slapped the bar and said, "*Come on. Come on. Come on.* How much is that fucking guy making?"

An outfielder for the Blue Jays snagged it and threw it hard and fast whence it came. Grady shook his head and took a sip of beer. He signaled the bartender for another. He did not seem the least bit drunk or tipsy. It might take a keg or two, as he appeared to be pushing about two-fifty.

"You never did say," he said.

"Say what?"

"Why McGee sent you."

"Jack didn't send me," I said. "I just heard you'd been in that church before the flashback. Before your friends were trapped."

He nodded. But the look on his face was not pleasant. It turned a bright shade of red as he swallowed hard. He shook his head several times to show his disappointment in me.

"I hoped you'd tell me what you saw down there," I said. "I know Mike Mulligan radioed that the fire seemed to have started in two directions. What do you think about that?"

The bartender took away his pint glass and wiped down the moisture left behind. He laid down a fresh pint as John Grady studied my face. He wore his hair shaggy and long over his eyebrows and covering his ears. "Why? Why does it matter? Arson looked into it. I mean, Jesus Christ. Who the fuck are you?"

I introduced myself.

"That name supposed to mean something?"

"Ever read *The Faerie Queen*?"

"Do I look queer to you?"

"I would never speculate on one's sexual orientation," I said. "But your hair is a little long."

"You wanna get popped in the mouth?" he said.

"Not really," I said. "I need it to drink beer."

"Me, too," he said. "But how about you change the freakin' channel and quit busting my nuts. Unknown origin means freakin' unknown. It means you can't wrap up causes in a neat little package for the insurance companies and the paper-pushers. That church was a hundred years old. Christ. Shit happens."

"*Shit happens* isn't working for Jack McGee."

"Like I said, his head is fucked up," Grady said. He downed half his glass. "Like I said, no one is at the wheel. It's the anniversary, you know? Next week. They're having some kind of memorial. There's talk of putting up a freakin' statue or something."

"And you'll be there?"

He looked at me as if I might be nuts, too. He shook his head. "I'm a Boston firefighter, what the fuck do you think? I don't know who you are or what you're trying to do. But you start pissing on the memory of these men and you'll get your ass stomped."

"Sometimes, after a while, small details add up."

"Leave it alone," Grady said. "My back doesn't work on a divine plan, like the sisters used to tell us."

"But did you hear Mulligan say the fire had spread independently from two sources?"

"He said a lot of things before he died," he said. "That ain't one of them. I heard his last words. They were about his brothers with him. Not the fucking fire."

"But it's possible?" I said.

"*Pfft*," Grady said. "Crap."

"You're one of the first on the scene," I said. "Did you hear of anyone running from the building before the fire?"

"It was late," he said. "Nobody was there. What are you getting at? Nobody but Jack McGee thinks this was arson and the guy is still running crazy and loose. If that makes him feel better, let him think it. But how about you just let me sit here and watch my team lose. Do you mind? Is that too much to fucking ask?"

"Not a bit."

I placed my business card next to his beer. Grady studied it for a moment, and without looking away from the game, ripped it into several pieces and tossed it down to the floor. He sipped the beer some more. A nameless vet for the Sox was up to bat.

It didn't take too long before he struck out, too.

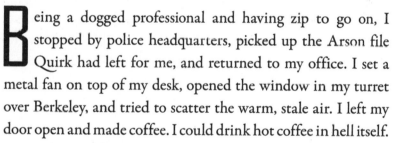

6

eing a dogged professional and having zip to go on, I stopped by police headquarters, picked up the Arson file Quirk had left for me, and returned to my office. I set a metal fan on top of my desk, opened the window in my turret over Berkeley, and tried to scatter the warm, stale air. I left my door open and made coffee. I could drink hot coffee in hell itself.

For the next hour, I read the reports on the Holy Innocents fire. There were interviews with the first responders, including Captain Collins and John Grady. There were interviews with witnesses, including a bartender just coming onto a shift, a taxi driver who'd first seen smoke coming from the basement, and a professional dog trainer named Janet Vera. There were lab tests on the type of char left on walls and support beams. Investigators ruled out electrical. Investigators ruled out accidental. Neither hide nor hair had been inside the building for weeks.

The coffee was ready. I poured a cup. Thick corned-beef sandwiches, tepid Guinness, and hot days were the trifecta to make me sleepy. I added a spoonful of sugar to my coffee and spun around in my chair. I read the autopsy reports for the men. They died of asphyxiation before being overcome by the flames. There were diagrams and maps showing where they'd fallen.

The file noted conversations between arson investigators and homicide detectives. The last entry came late last year.

Across Berkeley, in the new Houghton Mifflin Harcourt building, I watched a lithe woman in a red wrap dress walk from her desk, out her door, and then back to her desk again. Although I admired her commitment to personal fitness, I decided not to guess her age.

I waved to the young woman. She lifted her head and then quickly shut the blinds. *Ah, realize your youth while you have it.*

I finished the coffee and poured another half-cup. I thought about reading back through the file. Or perhaps cleaning my .38 or the .357 I kept in my right-hand drawer. I could open up a bottle of Bushmills. Or I could go to the gym and sweat.

I chose the latter, and within thirty minutes, I was sparring with Z at Henry's. We wore protective gear with eighteen-ounce gloves. We forwent the groin padding. That's how much I trusted Zebulon Sixkill.

He rocked a couple shots to my ribs. Even through the padding, I felt them.

"The force is strong with you," I said. "But you're not a Jedi yet."

"I will be soon," he said. "With the paper to prove it."

We circled each other in the ring. I stepped forward and

jabbed while he sidestepped the punch. I leveled a solid right against his head. His head reeled back.

"He's still got it," he said.

"You bet."

He took the opportunity to work out a nice combo on my body and went for the head. I ducked it and came up with a glancing blow in his stomach.

"What will Boston do without you?" I said.

"The women of Los Angeles need me," Z said. "But I'll finish what we started."

"And what if Hawk and I ever need you?" I said.

"Let's call L.A. a branch office," Z said. "I'm under the impression there's crime and corruption on the West Coast, too."

"Yes," I said. "I've heard rumors to that effect."

Z dropped his gloves a bit. Jab, cross, left uppercut, cross. The second cross connected with his head. Harder than he or I had expected. He stumbled back a couple steps. I backed up and circled. He smiled, shook his head, and came back for me. We'd trained for years and I'd miss him a great deal.

"Hawk said if you can't beat 'em, shoot 'em," Z said.

"Maybe," I said. "However, I've never known anyone who could beat Hawk."

"Or you?"

"Living?"

"Yeah."

"Nope."

"So when do you use a gun instead of your fists?" Z said.

"Only when necessary," I said. "Don't pull your gun if you're not willing to kill."

Z nodded. He stepped in and jabbed twice, shot a cross, and then followed with a hook. The hook shaved my ribs but, had it connected, might have proved painful.

"Sell the punch," I said. "Always sell the punch."

The timer buzzed, and we both grabbed the water bottles where we'd left them. We were both breathing hard and our T-shirts were soaked in sweat. Z took off his headgear and poured water over his black hair. He spit in a bucket and we both waited for the buzzer.

"One more round," I said. "Keep your hands up."

"I know," he said.

"The hardest lessons are the easiest to forget."

The buzzer sounded and again we circled each other.

They'd been burning shit for months now. What surprised them was how easy it had been. Of course, they had rules. You can't set a fire closer than fifty feet from a building. You can't set a fire near an occupied building. Nobody wanted to hurt anyone or do any real damage. They basically piled up junk in weedy lots and poured on the gasoline. Dumpsters were fun because they were self-contained and burned big and bold. At the end of January, they'd lit up the alleys off Storrow Drive and drove over the river to watch them burn. A nice orange glow off the trash every few blocks.

For Kevin, it'd been better than the Fourth of July.

"This is chickenshit stuff," Johnny said one night at the Scandinavian Pastry shop.

"It's what we wanted."

"This is like Halloween pranks," Johnny said. "I know this building in Mattapan. It's perfect."

This was back in the winter, and the idea of a nice big fire had sounded just about perfect. The building was an old triple-decker maybe a quarter-mile down from Norfolk Hardware and Home, where Kevin had worked in high school. Johnny brought a crowbar and they whacked themselves inside. Ray found them a couple threadbare tires to lean up against a wall. The whole place was like a spook house, like the Mickey Mouse cartoon where they were ghost catchers.

This was the night they'd come up with La Bomba. The idea for it was part Kevin's and part Johnny's. But what came of it was simple, basic, and beautiful. You fill a freaking Ziploc bag with kerosene, slip it into a brown paper bag, attach a matchbook with tape, and slide in a lit cigarette. The cigarette works like the fuse and you can make it long or short. By the time La Bomba went, they were halfway back to the donut shop. By the time the scanners went nuts, they were all tucked in at the back booth, munching on some plain glazed.

Drinking bad coffee as the Sparks Association—guys who were fans of the flame, too—dropped their dicks and grabbed their coats, all asking: "Hey? Hey, what's going on? Where is it?"

Johnny shook his head, reached for his coat, this one looking official, with fire patches from all over New England on it, and went out to his red Chevy Blazer, and Kevin to his Crown Vic. They all arrived back at the old triple-decker in Mattapan about the same time. Johnny had even bought a couple dozen donuts to hand out to the boys. He'd jumped in with the boys from Engine 53 and helped them move the hose as they fanned the roof of the building. Neighbors from down the street came to watch. Cops arrived.

Maybe thirty minutes later, Kevin felt Ray in full cop uniform at his elbow. Ray shaking his head. "You crazy fucks."

Big Ray was smiling. The idea that they'd boosted the game excited the hell out of him.

And it did for Kevin, too. They were doing something. They were bringing meaning and attention to Boston Fire. Someday, when he got on with BFD, he knew things would be different. The city would give the guys real equipment, proper firehouses, and the respect they deserved. This wasn't just about burning stuff. This was about his own future and the future for Boston.

"Hot, hot," Johnny said. "Wow. Can you take my picture?"

Kevin took Johnny's camera and stepped back. Johnny now wearing a firefighter helmet and the patch-covered coat. Ray ambled over and hugged him. In the background, the firemen worked to put out the blaze. They were sweating and breathing hard. But the practice was good for all of them.

Kevin took the shot and gave the boys a thumbs-up. That was the night Mr. Firebug was born.

7

The next morning, I waited at Flour Bakery near the Seaport for the Boston Fire Museum to open. I tried to use my time constructively by polishing off two cinnamon donuts. Simple, elegant, and perfect. At nine, a tall, lanky man with thinning black hair opened up the old brick firehouse and let me inside. He wore pleated khakis with sneakers and a sensible short-sleeved plaid dress shirt. He turned on the overhead fluorescent lights and a portable scanner by a cash register.

Vintage fire engines and horse-drawn pumps shared the wide space with plenty of old axes, and a collection of helmets hung from the rafters.

The man stood behind the counter and plucked a toothpick in the side of his mouth. He studied me through a pair of thick gold metal glasses with the mild manners of a local insurance agent. His name tag read ROB FEATHERSTONE.

Rob Featherstone, head of the Sparks Association, was one of the first at Holy Innocents.

I introduced myself. He gave me a skeptical look and said, "What's a private cop gotta do with any fire business? Fire business is for the fire department."

"I'm working with the police," I said. Sort of telling the truth. "Some people believe whoever torched the church is still out there setting fires."

"Who said the church was arson?"

"Arson doesn't have an official cause either way."

"I still don't see what that has to do with some private cop," he said. "Those Arson dicks are sharp. Real sharp. Smart as hell. What's your name again?"

"Spenser," I said. "With an *S*."

"Never hearda you."

"Unfortunate," I said.

"Why's that?"

"I'm huge in Japan."

"I really wish I knew something," he said. "But I'm just the guy handing out water and coffee to our boys. Like I said, I got no freakin' idea how that fire got started. I'm just the support team."

"Perhaps you might have something or someone," I said. "Even if it seems small."

"I was there all of two minutes before Pat Dougherty and his crew pulled up."

"Who else was there?" I said. "Did you notice anything strange about anyone at the scene?"

"You know how many weirdos like to watch fires?" he said. "Present company included."

He smiled. I kept my mouth shut.

He grinned and used his fingers to feather over his few remaining strands of black hair. "Must've been a hundred folks on Shawmut that night."

"How long did you stay?"

"All freakin' night," he said. "Never went home. I saw those boys run into the church and I was there when they brought 'em out. Goddamn it. I'll never forget that. That's what those men mean to this city. Running into a building to stop the fire, protect this neighborhood. That's why we do what we do. These guys give their lives. These aren't sport stars with million-dollar contracts. They do it 'cause they got honor and respect for this town."

"Especially this summer," I said. "It seems there's a fire every night."

"This is the most action the department has seen in a while. But most of it is a lot smaller than that church. Lots of Dumpsters. Abandoned buildings. Burning for show."

"The church was abandoned, too."

"That was almost a year ago," Featherstone said. "Christ, Mr. Spenser. I don't mean to be a jerk, but who thought you could do any better than the department?"

"If it was an accident," I said, "I can't help pinpoint the cause. But if it was something criminal, that's in my line of work. It takes a while to find a pattern in some random acts."

"Like I said, I don't think it was set," he said. "I know what arsons look like. We had like two dozen in the last couple of months. This was an old church and some wire crossed or some dumb bastard left a cigarette in that alley. I mean, who the hell would burn a church? You don't go to confession for that kind of crap."

The dispatcher advised of two minor injuries on Atlantic Avenue near the aquarium. Police were on scene and reported medical attention was needed. I leaned on the display case and looked down at some artifacts from the Cocoanut Grove fire of '42. I studied the news clippings and a menu from the old nightclub.

Featherstone walked around the table and joined me at the display. He swiveled the toothpick in his mouth and made a sighing sound.

"I once met the man who thought he'd done it," Featherstone said. "He'd been nothing but a kid, trying to change out a light-bulb. He lit a match to see what he was doing under a paper palm tree and *whoosh*. That fire burned hotter and faster than about anything in history. When the firemen got inside, they found people still sitting at their tables, cocktails in front of them. Bodies in perfect shape. Christ."

I nodded and let him talk.

"I think he replayed that event in his mind every damn day."

"From what you've heard, do you think there might've been two points of origin?"

"Boy, you don't quit, do you?" Featherstone said. He smiled and thought about it before shaking his head. "I mean, I can't be sure. When I got there it was mainly smoke. A lot of black smoke. Everything was coming from the basement and out that side alley. I didn't see anything in the sanctuary. But after Dougherty, Bonnelli, Mulligan, and Grady went in, I could see the big stained-glass window lit up with the fire. The fire had burned its way upstairs and into the sanctuary. But as far as two fires, I can't say. I guess we'll really never know."

"I hope that's not the case."

"I didn't leave that church until maybe two or three the next day. I was there when Dougherty's wife and two of his kids showed up. That's something I didn't want to see. You ever hear someone scream not out of fright but out of real animal pain? Stuff deep inside?"

"I'm afraid so."

"That's what it is," Featherstone said. He walked back around from the counter. A thick-calved woman in a blue dress and a husky kid in a tricorne hat bounded into the museum. The husky kid tried to crawl under the velvet ropes and onto a horse-drawn pump. "Hold on."

The husky kid made it as far as the wooden wheels before Featherstone told him to get back behind the ropes. Featherstone wandered back to me.

"I didn't get real close," he said. "Most of the fire I was working. I hate what happened to the guys. But shit, I'd do anything I could if some son of a bitch set it. But it's just a sad day, nothing more. Life sometimes doesn't make any sense."

"But if something changes," I said. I handed him my card.

"I promise," he said.

Unlike John Grady, he didn't toss it on the floor. Progress.

F ive days later, Boston Fire marked the year anniversary that Dougherty, Bonnelli, and Mulligan had died inside Holy Innocents. Outside the blackened shell of what had been the church, the chaplain prayed and everyone dropped their heads. It started to rain. Except for a few politicians, nobody opened an umbrella during the service to the fallen firefighters.

The whole South End went quiet. You could hear the wind and rain hitting the street.

The fire radio clicked on and a dispatcher read the men's names and time of the fire last year to the minute. Across Boston, sirens wailed. The skies then opened up and covered Shawmut Street in slanted sheets of water.

I pulled up the collar on my jacket and removed my hat. I stood back as the firefighters shook hands and hugged one another. Across the street, TV news trucks had set up, taking video from a respectable distance. After a few minutes, the fire trucks drove away. Dozens of firefighters lingered. A few of them were walking into a break in the fence line and going into the church.

"You making any progress?" McGee said.

"I interviewed four more first responders," I said. "And a half a dozen people who watched the church burn."

"Insurance?"

"Checked that out, too," I said. "Only one to benefit would be the archdiocese."

"They've done a helluva lot worse."

"Sure," I said. "But their payout wouldn't be even touching the historic value."

"Yeah," McGee said. "I guess they might've turned it into a steakhouse or something. Like that—"

"Smith and Wollensky," I said. "Of course the South End is growing that way. Maybe someday it will be a B and B for Labradoodles."

"First came the gays and all their arty-farty stuff and now the investment bankers with their Mercedes SUVs, complaining about all the city noise and traffic."

"Leave it to Gary Cooper and gays to clean up Dodge."

"This property is worth something to somebody," McGee said.

"Sure."

"Maybe worth more cleared than as some musty old church."

"I'm not so sure."

"I'll bet dollars to donuts," McGee said.

"Always an unwise bet," I said.

"Why?"

"I hold one in higher esteem."

"You tell me what, then," McGee said. "What else is there but greed? Someone wanted that church gone."

"Revenge," I said. "Extortion. An act of God."

"Revenge is looking good," McGee said. "But God would never let this happen. Not my God, anyway."

The rain slackened and I shook the water from my hat. It was a road hat for the Mississippi Braves that a friend down south had sent. Nearly identical to my Boston Braves hat except for the big *M* with a tomahawk through it. I watched the men coming and going from the break in the chain-link fence. I spotted John Grady. He had on a blue windbreaker but no hat. His long hair fell limp and wet over his big head as he gave me a hard stare.

After a few minutes, a tall man with a clipped mustache and wearing a black raincoat walked out.

"Oh, shit," McGee said.

I looked at McGee.

"Fucking Commissioner Foley," he said. "He's going to make a thing. Oh, Christ."

Foley shook a few more hands and then the commissioner walked on over. He wore a navy suit with a pale yellow tie. As he moved, you could see a small gold shield adorning his lapel. A smaller man in dress uniform walked in stride almost like a shadow.

He patted McGee's back, shook his hand, and eyed me. "Who's your friend?"

McGee introduced me.

"Yeah," he said. "I heard of you."

"My reputation stretches far and wide," I said.

"And that you've pissed a lot of people off."

"Yep."

"And caused a lot of folks in BPD a headache."

"Also true."

He put his hands in his pockets, looked down at the wet pavement. He shook his head as he stroked his mustache in thought. His sidekick stood back, eyeing me and Jack McGee with a raised chin.

"But I heard other things, too," Foley said.

I looked to Jack McGee. And he looked back at me, eyes widened.

"I know what you're up to," he said. "You been fucking sneaking around. Asking questions at my firehouses without coming to me first."

I nodded.

"You know these were good, honorable men?" Foley said. "And they died doing the right thing. They were helping people in this fucking city."

"I do."

"Then quit sneaking around," Foley said, putting a hand on my back. "You want to poke around? Fine. Then do it right. Come on down, I want you to see where they died."

McGee looked at me and let out a long, steady breath.

9

We followed an alley beside the Gothic stone church to a burned-out doorway. Inside, portable lights shone in the dark space. New wooden beams and studs shared space with charred and blackened wood. Foley pointed to the crossbeams overhead and the stone walls.

"The flashback happened here," he said. "This is where the mayday went out. We were pushing midlines down both steps. We had a company to the rear of the structure and out on Shawmut. I've never seen a fire burn so fast in my life."

Water dripped from the crossbeams, pinging puddles on the floor. Sawhorses, table saws, and piles of sawdust and scrap wood littered the basement. He walked to the stairwell, where his driver handed him a small Maglite.

Commissioner Foley cast light on charred spots along the

wall resembling an alligator's back. "This is deep char," he said. "This is where we believe the fire started."

"But we don't know how?"

"The first thing we do is try to rule out the obvious," he said. "We know this wasn't electrical. We can find no traces of an accelerant present. It kills you. But sometimes you never know. We know this is where the fire started and the spread just took over everything fast. All that was left was the stone. You think about something so small, a fucking spark hitting this wood and eating everything in its path like a fucking cancer."

"What about a second source?" I said. "Another spot it may have originated."

Foley stood. He looked to McGee and back at me, shaking his head. "I heard that shit, too. But it's not true. There's no evidence of multiple points of origin. Zip."

"Most of the church burned up so freakin' bad, how would we ever know?" McGee said.

Foley shrugged.

"Something burned up hot as hell at this very spot," McGee said. "Place was abandoned like half the buildings we're seeing right now. I don't care if there's a hundred points or just this one. No one does this shit and just stops cold."

Foley ran a hand over his jaw. He stared at McGee but didn't say a word.

"I'm sure you got your reasons," McGee said. His fat face was turning a bright red. "But I don't appreciate the way I been treated. Like I'm some kind of goofball for thinking the firebug did this. I loved Pat. He was my best friend. I was the one who had to call on his wife. Go get his kid at his goddamn soccer game. You know what it was like to hear that order to evacuate on the radio, knowing our guys were inside?"

Foley nodded. "Of course."

"Yeah," McGee said. His voice softening. "I know. I know."

"Can we agree it's suspicious?" I said.

"Of course it's suspicious," McGee said. "Arson's got some kind of evidence. And they found more at all the other fires."

Foley placed his hands inside his black rain slicker and shook his head. "Yeah?" he said. "Where'd you hear that, Jack?"

"Everyone in the department knows," McGee said. "Jesus Christ. You don't think firemen talk around the station? What else can we do but polish our engines."

"We start talking about a firebug and people start to panic," Foley said. "And then the crazies start joining in to copycat. You know how that shit goes."

"But you found something," I said.

"Yeah, yeah," Foley said. "We got something. But it's not enough yet. If you know something, you better let us know."

"Why don't you broadcast every shred you got to every reporter in this city? Put out a reward?"

"Like I said, we have to be careful about everything we do," Foley said. "This takes time."

"It's been a freakin' year," McGee said. "Give Spenser something to work off of. What can it hurt?"

"Look, if Spenser wants to poke around about this fire, I won't get in his way. Just promise me you'll share if you get something of use."

"Can I meet with investigators?" I said.

"That's up to them," Foley said. "But I'll ask."

"Arson is doing jack shit," McGee said. "They've had their thumb up their ass for the last year. I go down there to talk to them and they look like I just crapped in the sink. Why not let him talk to them?"

"Ease off," Foley said. "Let me see what I can do."

We walked back out into the light rain and fresh air. I took a deep breath, but could still smell the blackened wood and fire on my clothes. The short, squat man I'd seen before was waiting by a red Ford Explorer, holding a door open for Foley. The front plate had an official BFD tag.

Foley stopped for a moment to stare at McGee. "Is he as good as he says?"

McGee looked to me. "If he's half as good as his ego, it'll help."

"Jack speaks the truth," I said. "My ego is massive."

Foley gave me a nod and walked to the car. The car sped away and I was alone in the rain with Jack McGee.

"What the fuck was that?" he said.

"Cooperation?" I said.

"Maybe," he said. "Maybe not. Watch your ass. Anytime a jake leaves the ranks, it makes me nervous."

10

Susan was still in session. I let myself in, took Pearl for a short walk, and as a reward popped the top on a Lagunitas IPA. Z had introduced me to the beer, as it hailed, like him, from the West Coast.

I sat on Susan's back deck and tossed tennis balls to Pearl. Even though Pearl was aging, she could retrieve better than Irving Fryar. A tennis ball wasn't quite the pros, but she didn't seem to mind. I let Pearl back in the house for some water, removed my knit shirt, and started Susan's push lawnmower. Her diminutive lawn had gotten shaggy.

The whole thing took less than twenty minutes.

After I finished, I helped myself to another beer as a reward and sat again with Pearl on the back deck. I had on Levi's, a pair of running shoes, and sunglasses. I must have looked rakish when Susan walked onto the back deck and eyed the lawn. Freshly cut grass smelled of summer.

"How much do I owe you?" she said.

"I've seen movies that started off like this."

"How about you prune the bushes and we'll talk."

I smirked but restrained comment. Susan only shook her head.

Susan had already changed from shrink garb into a pair of khaki shorts and a lightweight gray T-shirt with a tiny square pocket. She wore her hair on top of her head in a bun and no shoes. Her large, dark eyes were luminous.

"How about an early dinner at Alden and Harlow?" I said.

"Or a later dinner at the Russell House Tavern?" she said.

"Equally enticing," I said. "Does a later dinner imply we enjoy a matinee?"

She sat with me on the steps, took a sip of the beer, and handed it back. I was pretty sure she was surveying my landscaping skills. "I knew you were angling when you cut the grass."

"Did you notice the patterns I mowed?" I said.

"Amazing."

"Out front, I cut a little heart with an arrow through it."

"What will the neighbors say?"

"It's Cambridge," I said. "They find us as eccentric as every-one else."

"Okay," she said. "But only on one condition."

"I wear a lacy thong?"

"Ha," she said. "Just don't mess up my hair, big guy."

I threw the tennis ball long and far for Pearl, stood, and opened the back door wide for Susan. She walked on ahead of me into the coolness of her house and tossed her T-shirt into my face.

"Race you upstairs," she said.

T he next morning, I called on Father Conway at the Immaculate Conception Church in Revere. Conway was a youngish guy, mid-thirties, with a long, thin face and close-cropped dark hair. He wore a clerical collar on his clergy shirt and black-framed glasses that we'd called birth-control specs in the service. He looked a lot like a young Fred Gwynne, minus the bolts in his neck.

"At first I was thankful the church was abandoned," Conway said. "But then they brought those men out in bags. I'll never forget the firefighters standing at attention as they loaded them in ambulances. It was a horrible morning."

Up front stood the requisite organ and an all-star lineup of saints along the walls, holy water in a marble baptismal font, and a large wooden cross draped in white. The carpet in the sanctuary was very old, the color of a putting green. The church smelled as fresh as a grandmother's coat closet.

"I was there yesterday," I said. "For the memorial."

"I wanted to attend," Conway said. "But I had two funerals this morning. And a wake tonight."

"Plenty of security in your work," I said.

"And yours," he said. Smiling. "It's been a busy and hard summer. When I counsel people I often talk about how our troubles could be much worse. Often it's the small things that pressure us most."

"Life," I said. "Just a temporary condition."

Conway smiled at me and nodded. I sat in the second row of pews and he sat in the first. His left arm was stretched out lengthwise as he turned around to talk with me. He looked very relaxed and at home in the musty old church.

"Did you ever hear any theory from the arson investigators?"

"No."

"Any theories of your own?"

"With a church that old, I would assume something electrical," he said. "I don't believe anyone ever found out. And it seems now they never will."

"Investigators have ruled out most everything," I said. "Including electrical."

"Arson?"

"Some believe it was set," I said. "But there's no evidence. The worry is that if it was arson, the same person is loose and setting new fires."

"I don't know why anyone would set fire to the church," he

said. "Plenty of people were very upset about it being sold. They wanted it protected."

I nodded and tried to give the impression I'd known that all along. I kept nodding so he wouldn't suspect.

"The archdiocese had been wanting it shut down for years," he said. "That church was started by German immigrants, but for the last twenty years was mainly an outreach for the homeless and drug abusers. I'd been there for only three years, but we were growing, bringing in young families in the South End. It was becoming a viable church again. As you know, some parts of the South End transition slower than others."

"So why would they close it?"

"After all the scandals and our numbers dwindling," he said, "we needed the money. This isn't your parents' Catholic Church. Things have changed a great deal."

"I had expected to become more devout as I grew older. Somehow that hasn't happened."

"*A Farewell to Arms,*" he said. "The old man playing pool with the young lieutenant."

"A literate priest."

"I took an American lit course while at BC," he said. "Some things actually stick. May I ask, are you Catholic, Mr. Spenser? You look to be of Irish stock."

"My mother was Catholic," I said.

"Did she take you to Mass?"

"She died in childbirth," I said. "Her brothers, my uncles, took me some when we moved to Boston. My father had lost all faith. Except what he found in whiskey bottles."

He nodded.

"Can you think of any reason someone would want to burn the church?" I said. "Did anyone in the neighborhood hold a grudge or ever make threats?"

"No."

"May I ask who would want to buy an old church?" I said. "Except another religious group."

"Holy Innocents was the last piece of a block someone needed for some kind of major redevelopment," he said. "I guess they thought no one would notice the razing of a hundred-year-old historic structure. Or at least didn't care."

"Do you recall the buyer?"

"I'm sorry," he said. "Those decisions are made by men in pointy red hats."

"Perhaps you might find out for me?"

He studied my face, seeming to take me more seriously now that he knew I'd been raised Catholic. "That should be fairly easy. If you don't mind waiting."

I sat there in the hard pew for a half-hour before Conway returned with a name of a development company and a phone number. I thanked him. "I also appreciate you not asking how long it's been since my last confession."

"That long?"

I smiled. "Father, I don't believe you'd even been born."

Herbie Wu agreed to meet me outside his real estate office
near Copley Square. I waited on a park bench next to the
turtle statues, well within the shadow of the Trinity
Church. I spotted Wu as he walked across the square. Not because he was Asian American, but because he looked like a
multimillionaire real estate mogul named Herbie. He had on
tan shorts, a light blue dress shirt, and a bright purple jacket.
His sunglasses looked like they cost more than my SUV. The
shorts-and-jacket combo was a bit disconcerting.

I rose, introduced myself, and shook hands. He was short,
with small hands and slick hair. He had one of those soul-patch
things under his lower lip.

"You know some important people, Mr. Spenser."

"A few."

"Fast Eddie Lee?"

"I knew you did a lot of business in Chinatown."

"Everyone in Chinatown must do business with Mr. Lee."

"Traditional?" I said.

"Not really," he said. "Let's say necessary."

I nodded.

"And now you do a lot of business in the South End?" I said.

"Some," he said. "But not as much as I'd like. The South End has grown too expensive even for me. Property is being held hostage. Too rich. Even with some investors from back in the old country."

"Where'd you grow up, Mr. Wu?"

He grinned. "Quincy."

I smiled. Pigeons fluttered away from two young boys chasing them. A man playing an accordion had set up nearby and played the latest pop hits. The man didn't have much talent but seemed enthusiastic.

"Last year you were about to purchase Holy Innocents," I said.

"Where did you hear that?" he said.

"From a holy man."

"Did this holy man tell you they still wanted me to pay after the fire?"

"Nope."

"I don't pay for damaged property," he said. "The contract was still being looked after by lawyers. We had kept it out of public record because *The Globe* would have had a field day with development on a historic property."

"And what had you planned to do with a hundred-year-old church, Mr. Wu?" I said.

He rubbed the insignificant tuft of hair under his chin. "Hmm," he said. "May I ask why you want to know? I don't often air business in public with strangers."

"Especially with strangers introduced by crooks?"

"Are you saying Fast Eddie Lee is not a legitimate business-man in Boston?" Wu said. He smiled. "I'm shocked."

"Heavens, no."

Herbie rested his elbows on his bare legs. I noticed he wasn't wearing socks with his suede loafers. I didn't pass judgment. I'm a no-socks man myself.

"Condos," he said.

"You were going to turn an old church into a condo?"

"Well," he said. "You couldn't tear it down. It was going to be part of a much larger development. I had plans for an entire stretch of what we developers call mixed-use. I don't know if you've seen the church, but it's not in the hippest section of the South End."

"And now?"

"I walked away," he said. "I've gone on to other projects. In business you have to weigh your costs and benefits."

"Too high a cost?"

"Way too high."

"That had nothing to do with rebuilding after the fire?"

He shook his head. "To be honest, the fire would have helped me out," Wu said. "Less red tape and meetings with the Planning Commission. Can you imagine how much flack I'd get from preservationists? We'd already been working on a plan to retain as much of the edifice as possible while working around it."

"So why get out?" I said.

Across from the public library, a large bandstand was being erected. A group of tourists on bicycles cut through the park, all smartly wearing helmets. The guide stopped and pointed out some of the important sites around them. I thought about waving but decided to keep a low profile.

Herbie Wu shook his head. "It's been nice meeting you, Mr. Spenser," he said.

I didn't move. "Just what did Mr. Lee tell you about me?"

"He said you've been a pain in his ass."

"Did he say that in English or Chinese?"

"I only speak a little Chinese," Wu said. "He said it in English."

"And what else?"

"Be careful of what I say," he said. "But you can be trusted."

I nodded. The tourists on bicycles pedaled off toward Boylston Street. The accordion player had launched into a horrific version of "Squeeze Box" by The Who. I might've preferred "Lady of Spain."

Wu stood, the wind ruffling his expertly barbered hair. He checked his smartphone, bored, and offered his hand. I stood and shook it.

"You weren't wanted in the neighborhood?"

Wu didn't answer.

"If it wasn't money?"

"It was money," Wu said. "Everything is money. But this isn't Chinatown. I pay taxes. I don't have to pay protection."

"Who?"

He shook his head. "I don't think so."

"I promise you I'll leave you far out of this," I said. "I only need a name. I walk away and you'll never hear from me again."

"This wasn't my first encounter with that bastard," Wu said. "Or I suspect my last."

I waited. I could tell he wasn't a fan of whoever may have smoked him out of the South End.

"Doesn't matter if you're from Beijing or Bedford," he said. "Business is the same everywhere. And right now, if you want to set up a lemonade stand in that part of the South End, you got to pay off Jackie DeMarco. It's too close to Southie."

I nodded.

"You've met him?"

"Quite recently," I said. "And we did not part on good terms."

"I have no proof," Wu said. "But his people came to me two weeks before the fire. They knew of the impending sale. I told them I would not pay a nickel."

"Bingo."

"Excuse me."

"I always say that when I move down the food chain."

"Be careful, Mr. Spenser," he said. "This is a man without boundaries or ethics."

"Criminals rarely possess those traits."

"The same might be said about developers."

"Depends on what they develop."

"You promise to leave my name out of this?"

I agreed. Wu nodded and walked away. I tipped the accordion player two bucks as I left.

I t was June now, hot as hell, and Johnny had the crazy idea to hit an old mattress factory in Dorchester. The building was big and brick, with a billboard on a far wall showing a little girl snuggled up for bedtime. The girl's blanket had little moons and stars, reminding Kevin of when he'd been a kid. He remembered how his mom used to come in at night, tuck him in, make him feel safe before he dozed off. Even now that he was a grown man, she looked out for him. Looking over him. Although she didn't know everything, she'd believe what he was about to do was right.

"You brought it?" Kevin said.

Johnny looked at him like he was a freakin' idiot. "No. I forgot it. Hell, yes, I got it. It's in the trunk. I made six of them. I figured with three of us working, we could spread them around."

"What about a security guard?" Kevin said.

"Not tonight," Johnny said. "Off on Friday night. Besides, they don't make them here anymore. They ship 'em in from China or somewhere. It's just a fucking warehouse now. Ready to burn."

"How do we get in?" Kevin said.

"Back loading dock," he said, holding up his crowbar. "A cheap deadbolt on a clasp. Snap, crackle, pop."

A whoop-whoop siren came from deep down the alley and the men turned. A patrol car rolled by slowly with its lights on, a spot flicking back and forth over the road and up onto the brick warehouse, finally falling on their faces, burning their eyes. "Christ," Johnny said.

The patrol car stopped, and in the blinding light, a door opened and a shadow of a cop got out. "Show me your hands, fucknuts."

"Screw you, Ray," Johnny said. "You about gave me a fucking heart attack."

"You'd have to have a heart first," Ray said, snorting. "And a dick."

Ray turned off the spotlight and followed them over to Johnny's car. Johnny popped the trunk to show six brown paper bags set neat in a row, as if ready for lunchtime. Each of the men grabbed two bags. Johnny ran down the layout of the place where they were most likely to get more bang for the buck. The third floor was pretty much empty, but there was a room with a lot of scraps and trash in it.

The fourth floor was gold, with old mattresses stacked ten feet high and ready to burn.

"I hope you know what you're doing," Ray said.

"Yes, Officer," Johnny said, flicking at his badge. "But do you?"

"I just want to do some good," Ray said, heading toward the loading dock. He was just like the rest of them, would give up his left arm to be a firefighter. If he hadn't gotten on with the cops first, he'd still be waiting for them to call his number. Instead, you had to be a fucking veteran, the son of a fireman, or some dummy minority. All of them could add so much to the department. All of them wanting to fight fires since they were kids.

As the big rolling door slid back, Kevin recalled that little room in Lynn where he'd grown up. The stars and the moons on his blanket and the little red fire hat on the hook by the door. She was so sure he'd be part of it someday. The happiest days were after they'd look for fires, both of them coming up smelling like smoke, talking about what they'd seen and heard. Never talk about his father. He was nothing. He could never be a man like those in the department. Not like what Kevin would become.

Kevin carried a sack in each hand and walked into the darkness, a small bit of light shining through the dirty industrial windows. He was to set both on the first floor. Johnny would call them on the walkie-talkie when it was time to set it off.

Two years since he turned in his application. Two years of calling every month to see where he stood on the list.

Still fifty ahead of him. None of them ready for the challenge like he was.

Kevin sat on his haunches in the middle of the desolate building. It was warm inside, with trapped heat from the long summer day. He lit a cigarette and smoked a bit, taking in the big, cavelike space that smelled of mold and stagnant water. New boxed mattresses stacked ten to fifteen high as far as he could see. He watched the glowing tip of the cigarette and took a breath. Everything just seemed endless.

"Now," Johnny said. "Do it!"

13

"Some might deem this entrapment," I said.

Hawk said, "Heard it was Give a Honkie a Donut Day."

"Is that a thing?" I said.

"Is now."

I reached into the box from Kane's and selected a cinnamon sugar. The selection was dazzling. Toasted coconut. Oreo sprinkles. Maple bacon. Since Kane's had come from Saugus to the Financial District, I'd been unfaithful to my old standby.

"Who eats meat on donuts?" Hawk said.

"It's not just meat," I said. "It's bacon. Bacon makes everything better."

Hawk nodded. We leaned against the brick wall above the marina at Rowes Warf. Hawk selected a coconut, careful not to get any shavings on his fitted T-shirt. It was the kind that wicked away sweat. In the late-afternoon heat, his face and bald head shone with perspiration.

"What's in it for me?" Hawk said.

"C'mon," I said. "How'd you know I needed a favor?"

Hawk just looked at me. He reached for a donut and took off a healthy bite.

"Arson case," I said. "Looks like it's circling back to Jackie DeMarco."

"Hot dog."

"And given our history with Jackie," I said. "Well. You know."

"Ha," Hawk said.

I ate a donut, trying to make it last, and stared out into the harbor. It was late afternoon and the water was filled with motorboats, little speedboats, and yachts. The water ferry from Logan skitted along, churning waves, cutting a path to the Boston Harbor Hotel.

"You think Jackie's still holding a grudge?"

"I shot two of his best men."

"If they were his best," I said, "he might've traded up."

Hawk nodded. He wore a pair of dark Oakleys, but I felt a hard stare behind the Oakleys. He'd set his gym bag on the brick wall, the zipper open, showing a pair of blue Lonsdale mitts.

"Insurance racket?"

"Nope," I said. "Jackie's casting a hand over some property in a bad part of the South End."

"Someone wouldn't pay up." Hawk continued to stare from behind his sunglasses. As he chewed, a fleck of shaved coconut dropped on his shirt. He flicked it away as if it were a gnat. "We need to pay Jackie a visit?"

"Not yet," I said. "I'm still in the gathering phase. I'd prefer him not knowing about it."

Hawk shook his head. "Someone like DeMarco ain't stopping with what he got," he said. "If he's moving out of Southie, man has delusions of grandeur. Wants to be his daddy or the new Joe Broz."

"He'll have to work on his wardrobe."

Hawk snorted.

"Only one?" I said. I nodded to the box with ten left.

"The rest are for you, white boy," Hawk said. "After all, it's your day."

"You ever hear anything about DeMarco burning people out?"

"Not my line of work, babe," he said. "I'm not into subtlety."

Hawk reached for another donut anyway, a maple-bacon one. He smiled as he ate. It must've been good. Hawk rarely smiled.

"Vinnie?" I said.

Hawk licked his fingers. "Or Gino Fish."

"Gino isn't what he used to be," I said. "But Vinnie is more."

I rested forearms on the high wall looking over the harbor. When Hawk and I had been young, it was sometimes tougher outside on the street than in the boxing gym. A man had to walk with purpose if he wanted to keep his wallet. Now the expressway was a Greenway and blight was a thing of the past.

Hawk hoisted his gym bag on his shoulder and left. I turned

and kept looking out at the Boston Harbor, the light sailboats zipping to and fro without much effort. The sails full of wind and energy, speed, and power.

In an effort to double my strength, I reached into the box Hawk had left for a second donut. Always prepared.

Vinnie Morris ran the business from an old bowling alley
right off the Concord Pike. When I walked in, a fat guy in
a Hawaiian shirt was cleaning rental shoes and singing an
old Bonnie Tyler song. "'Turn around, bright eyes,'" he sang.
And then he continued the chorus. He didn't need to contem-
plate his day job.

He stopped singing, looked me over from head to toe, and
then pointed up the staircase. The staircase was wide, metal,
and mid-century mod. There were plastic plants and a painted
mural of a ball hitting a strike. The pins exploding around it.
The fat man kept on singing the same lines as I climbed the
steps.

Upstairs, Vinnie sat at an empty bar, talking on a landline.
Two cell phones sat near a spiral notebook. A cigarette twirling
smoke up into a paddle fan.

He pointed to a nearby seat. I walked behind the bar and helped myself to a cup of coffee. Last time, he'd offered me grappa. I'd accepted and hence learned my lesson.

"Yeah, yeah, yeah. Okay. Okay. Fucking do it," Vinnie said into the phone. He turned to me. "Hello, Spenser. Why don't you just help yourself?"

"Service with a smile."

He hung up the phone.

"Bar opens at five."

"I never knew the bar to be open."

"It's a new thing," he said. "I mean, what the hell. Why not?"

Vinnie was the most distinguished-looking thug I'd ever met. Salt-and-pepper hair. Clean-shaven lantern jaw. A medium-sized guy in middle age who kept himself trim. During a divorce, his wardrobe had devolved into track suits, but in the past couple years he was back to his old self. Today, he wore a tailored navy linen shirt, with linen pants the color of vanilla ice cream. An alligator had died to make his belt and shoes.

I sipped some coffee. Terrible, but coffee nonetheless.

"What do you know about Jackie DeMarco?" I said.

"We've been over this before," he said. "Right before Hawk shot a couple of his guys down in Southie."

"We had a misunderstanding."

"My advice is to leave alone whatever you have in mind," he said. "DeMarco walked away from the flaming pile of shit you started. He won't do it again."

"I know he's into stolen property and drugs," I said.

Vinnie shrugged.

"How about arson?"

Vinnie looked away and scratched the back of his neck. He pulled his notebook close, scribbled in some figures, and then turned back to me. He picked up his half-burned cigarette, took a puff, and squinted through the smoke.

"Maybe," he said. "If money's involved, he'd set his mother's house on fire."

"And who might do that work for him?"

"What, you got some kind of Symphony Road situation?" he said. "That was a long, long time ago. No one burns for insurance anymore. Property in this town is worth too much fucking money."

"So I've been told," I said. "This was about turf."

"Someone pissed him off?"

I nodded. Vinnie raised his eyebrows.

"And that didn't scare you in the least?"

I shrugged. Never being a fast learner, I drank some more coffee. It was late afternoon. I could use the fuel.

"Only one guy I know," Vinnie said. "Worked for Broz back in the day. I hear he's still called out of retirement from time to time. A real artist with burning shit."

"A name?"

"Listen, why don't you come see me sometime when you or Hawk don't need me doing work for you," he said. "We could bowl a few games. Have some beer. A few laughs."

"You really want that?"

Vinnie lit a new cigarette. "Hell, no," he said. "What I want is for you to know what you're getting into. Learn something for me. I've moved from the field into management. I get up late, drink coffee, read the newspaper. I make some calls and

I'm done. After all these years, I got out while the getting is good. Unnerstand?"

"Not many Thug Emeritus positions."

"Check Harvard," Vinnie said. "I wouldn't put any crazy shit past them."

I nodded. I waited. Either Vinnie would give me a name or he wouldn't. He looked me over and said, "Ever hear of Tommy Torcelli? Aka Tommy Torch?"

"Sounds like he used to front a doo-wop group."

"Ha, ha," Vinnie said. "He used to work as a mechanic in Dorchester. Down by Fields Corner. He was the go-to guy for a long time. I heard he got busted for some kind of kiddie-porn thing. He's a true sicko in every way."

"Boy, I sure would love to meet him."

"I think he's still in the can," Vinnie said. "But I know he did business with Jackie and his old man. If someone wanted something burned, Tommy Torch would be on his speed dial."

I nodded.

"The guy can burn two city blocks and make it look like a firefly farted. You know?"

"A true genius."

"Yeah," Vinnie said. His cigarette bopped in his lips. "What got burned?"

"A Catholic church in the South End."

"The one where those firefighters died?"

I nodded.

"Jesus Christ."

"Exactly."

"What's the world coming to?" Vinnie said. "Joe Broz did a

lot of bad things. Killed a lot of people. But he'd never have burned a church. Or hurt a Boston firefighter."

"The new generation," I said. "Thugs without ethics."

Vinnie made a couple calls. I finished the coffee while watching the afternoon traffic jam up on the pike. After ten minutes, he'd arranged for a meet with Tommy Torcelli at Walpole. Vinnie said he and Tommy Torch went way back.

"How far?" I said.

"Far."

"Does he have ethics?"

"The man can't even spell *ethics*."

"Can he be trusted?"

"Nope."

"Good to know." I gave him a soft salute with two fingers and descended the stairs.

MCI Cedar Junction at Walpole was a quick yet not scenic drive from Boston on Route 128 South. The next morning, I made it in a little over an hour. The security process took a bit longer. Morning visitation was nearly done before I met Tommy Torch face-to-face through the glass. We had about twenty minutes to exchange pleasantries.

"I know you."

"Yeah?" I said.

"You're the guy that killed Fran Doerr," he said.

"Aw, shucks."

"He was an asshole," Tommy said. "Never liked the fucking guy. I like Vinnie. When Vinnie walked behind Broz, you knew where you stood."

"True."

"And Vinnie likes you."

"Vinnie and I have a mutual respect."

"He don't work with that queer Gino no more," he said. Tommy nodded for effect. "Runs his own affairs."

The guy gave me the creeps. His thin white skin was dotted with age spots. His face was small, skeletal, with bright blue eyes, his white and wispy hair pasted flat in long, useless strands. But no one looks good in an orange jumpsuit. It was very hard to pull off with style.

"So what can you do for me?" he said. "You wanna know something? Right?"

"I don't think we'd get along socially."

"I want a reduced sentence. This thing they got me for is junk. It wasn't even my computer. Someone set me up."

"I thought they caught you in the act?" I said. "With your pants around your ankles in Moakley Park?"

"Yeah," he said. "Well. I did that. Sure. But the other stuff. The added charges that keep me in here. That's not true."

If only the world's smallest violin were handy. Even with the Plexiglas separating us, our words exchanged only through a phone line, I felt the direct need to take a shower.

"I heard Jackie DeMarco had a church in the South End torched last year," I said. "You know anything about it?"

"I've been in jail for two years."

"I know," I said. "But I heard you'd been Jackie's go-to guy before you got popped."

"Maybe," he said. "I knew his old man a lot better. His old man was something. Used to run most of the city before Broz set him up. Drank espresso at a little table on Prince Street every morning. Funny how them things work. Everyone in this world is trying to cut you off at your knees. You know what? What I did was wrong. But I got popped for pissing off the wrong people. It was a setup. I got a sickness. People knew it. They used it as a fucking tool."

"I don't care," I said. "I want to know about the church fire."

He sat back and rubbed his face. He tried futilely to assemble a bit of dignity. But Elvis had left that building long ago. Tommy had few options, and this was probably his best chance since he'd landed back at Walpole.

"I read about it," he said. "In all the fires I set, I never had one fireman hurt. My fires burned right. They were places that needed to be torched, abandoned shit boxes for insurance cashout. I just made it look like it was an accident. Electrical and all that. Sometimes I'd cover a rat with kerosene and let it loose in the walls."

"Lovely," I said. "But who would Jackie use?"

"Nobody is gonna admit torching a place that killed no firefighter."

"Three," I said.

"I never killed no firefighter."

"You said that."

"You catch that guy and he gets life," he said. "If he's lucky. If he's unlucky, Boston Fire will find him first."

"I need a name," I said. "I'll take care of the rest."

"I don't want no part of this," he said. "I mean, I give you a name and then you go beat the crap out of someone. I mean, I got my own personal fucking code."

"Sure," I said. "If not, we're just a wild beast lost in this world."

"Huh?"

"Or at least some guy with lollipops in his pants."

"Fuck you, Spenser," he said. "I took this meet out of respect for Vinnie. If you don't want to do business, I got to get back to watching a bunch of blacks kill each other over shootin' hoops."

"You help me with this thing and I'll let the DA know," I said. "It's up to them what they do with you."

"I got people doing that for me already."

"I'm sure you're reforming every day here," I said. "Maybe you'll walk out of Walpole a clean and righteous man."

"I don't need this," Tommy said. He was about to hang up the phone. "I don't need to waste my time with the crap. Come back if you got a deal."

"How many visitors have you had lately?" I said. "It took a lot of effort to get a meet."

Tommy dropped the phone in a loose hand. He stared at me and thumbed his nose. He stared for a bit. I stared back. He was ugly and it wasn't easy.

"I help and you put in a good word?"

"The world is round," I said.

"How do I know I can trust you?"

"Because Vinnie said so," I said. "And because I'm not making you any promises."

Tommy took in a long breath. He looked worn out and beat. He rubbed his scruffy face and sat up straight in the hard plastic chair. "Let me see what I can do and I'll be in touch."

"You know how to find me?"

"I got your number."

"No promises."

"How about we quit talking," Tommy Torch said, "before I change my fucking mind."

By early afternoon, I returned to Boston only to find two ugly guys blocking my apartment building's doorway.

I might have walked around them. But one was John Grady and he was very fat. He also looked pissed-off. On the upside, he seemed to be sober and clean-shaven, his thick hair washed and styled. Grady had on a green T-shirt that read IT'S OUR FUCKIN' CITY. His friend was younger and in better shape. He was balding, with the rest shaved down to nearly nothing, wearing a black Gold's Gym tank and workout shorts. He was a bodybuilder with bloated muscles and puffy veins. His pinprick black eyes radiated as much intelligence as a lab rat's.

"You boys soliciting for the Jimmy Fund?" I said.

"You were down in the South End for the service," Grady said. "Trying to make trouble on a big day."

"How'd I make trouble?"

"Poking around," he said. "Asking questions. Talking shit with the commissioner."

Grady looked to the Michelin Man. Michelin Man staggered his stance. He stared at me with little eyes. He had a scar on one massive shoulder where he'd had a shoulder repaired. Lots of juicers had that problem. He looked to me and said, "Mmm."

"No one needs this shit," Grady said. "I don't need you bothering me at the pub. And no firefighters need you poking around on a sacred day."

"When should I poke around?"

"You got no business."

"That's where you're wrong," I said. "Trouble is my business."

"Like I told you," he said. "People are waiting in line to stomp your ass."

Michelin Man said "Mmm" again. His repertoire was dazzling. I waited for him to launch into the soliloquy from Hamlet.

"That line is long and winding," I said. "Past efforts have proven futile."

"What?"

"Futile," I said. "It means it's not worth attempting to threaten me or fight me. I'm tired and have planned a late breakfast. You boys don't look like you could make it to the Public Garden without a lot of sweat and sucking wind."

"Wanna bet?"

"I'm trying to help," I said.

"I'll toss you right in the garbage," the young guy said.

I shrugged. He took a fast step toward me, grabbing my arm. I pivoted off my right foot and landed a hard left in his soft gut. He made an *oof* sound and attempted to tackle me around the waist. I rammed his bald head into a brick wall and he slumped to the ground.

"John," I said, "unless you have some secrets, I'm working for you, too. Now, you can attempt to accost me and we could dance around Marlborough. The neighborhood watch might complain, as this type of behavior is frowned upon in the Back Bay. But I'd grow bored and tired. I have linens to change."

"*Pfft,*" he said. Grady spit on the sidewalk. Michelin Man was on his ass.

"Or," I said, "I'll buy you brunch. There's a nice place down the street. They even let you chain your pets outside."

Grady looked to his friend, sucking air. His bald head had started to bleed. I leveled my eyes at him and crossed my arms over my chest. If he didn't move, I might just start singing "If You Knew Susie, Like I Know Susie." I started to hum.

"'Oh, what a girl,'" I said, under my breath.

"What?" Grady said.

"Your call, John."

He seemed to think about it for a moment and then nodded to the Michelin Man. Michelin Man called me a few choice words and shuffled back to his car. We watched him go and then drive off in a beat-up Chevy sedan.

"Let's walk," I said.

We followed the Public Garden along Beacon and took a left on Charles to the Paramount. I bought Grady a stack of blueberry pancakes. I had the huevos rancheros with fresh-squeezed OJ and black coffee. Creature of habit. The afternoon was soft and warm. They'd opened up the windows fronting Charles.

"To recap," I said. "What's your problem with me?"

Grady hadn't touched his food. "You got no business."

"You said that," I said. "But if that stopped me, I wouldn't be very good at my job."

"This is Arson's case," he said. "They don't need you tracking shit through their house."

"A good metaphor, but far from accurate," I said. I reached for the coffee.

"A guy like you ain't in it for no one but themself."

"That's why you agreed to break bread with me?"

"Maybe I was fucking hungry."

I raised my eyebrows. Hard to argue with bulletproof logic.

"I think you have some kind of beef with Jack McGee and this doesn't have anything to do with you or me," I said. "Or even Dougherty, Bonnelli, and Mulligan."

"McGee is an asshole."

"Doesn't change what he believes."

"We never got along," Grady said. "We worked together six years ago. I never wanted to be on the same shift with him. He liked to piss me off. Always complaining and making trouble."

"How's he making trouble now?"

His mouth was full with a slab of blueberry pancake. I held up my hand to let him know he could finish chewing. I sipped on some coffee and added a half-packet of sugar.

"He didn't tell you?"

"Tell me what?"

"Come the fuck on," Grady said.

I shook my head. I waited. When in doubt, be quiet, let them talk. People like to fill the silence. I cut into the huevos rancheros. If there was any logic to the world, this breakfast would hang at the MFA.

"He didn't say?" Grady said. "No shit?"

"None at all."

"It's my fault."

I looked up. There was a lot of chatter and hum around us. People laughing and talking. Silverware clanging as small tables were cleared. New customers hustled for a seat once they got their food.

"How?" Oh, Spenser. Master interrogator.

"I killed them," Grady said. His face had drained of color and his blue eyes had grown very large. He breathed in and out of his mouth. He'd had only a few bites of pancake, and as he reached down for the coffee, his hand produced a slight tremble. "Jack knew. Jesus. He didn't say that? Isn't that what this is all about?"

I shook my head.

"Laying the blame," he said. "He wanted me to be exposed. I broke down that door, let in all that air. I wasn't listening to the radio chatter. I just fucking bust through that office. When that room opened up. All that fucking oxygen. *Whoosh*. That fire came up hard and fast. I got knocked back. My ears were burned and back broke. But, shit, I got out. I was pulled out. But. Oh, holy hell. Jesus. Jack? Jack didn't say?"

Grady was crying. I always had a hard time watching big men cry. I saw my father cry only twice. Both times scared the hell out of me.

"That's not your fault," I said.

"Bullshit," he said. "It's in a report. But it was kept quiet."

"McGee doesn't want you," I said. "He wants the men who set this. He thinks it's this firebug who's driving the department crazy."

"That's it?" Grady said.

I nodded. He wiped his face and blew his nose. It sounded like an out-of-tune trumpet. "What'd Arson tell you?"

"Zip," I said.

Grady rubbed his face. He nodded. "But you know they got a tape?" he said. "A surveillance tape of some bastard running from the church. Christ. I know for a fact they been sitting on that for a year."

The Arson squad kept separate offices from headquarters in an old firehouse on Mass Ave, blond brick with twin bay doors for investigators' vehicles. I found a battered red door and took the stairs up to the second floor. The captain knew I was coming and he buzzed me in.

He was a big man, bigger than me, with gray hair and a drooping Sam Elliott mustache. He met me at the landing with a panting yellow Lab at his side. I liked him right away. His name was Teddy Cahill. His dog's name was Galway.

"Did I mention I can do an amazing rendition of 'Danny Boy'?"

"I'm glad someone can," Cahill said. "Went to a wedding this weekend and none of the kids knew the words. It broke my heart."

"Every generation laughs at the old fashions, but religiously follows the new."

"You ain't fucking kidding."

We stood in the kitchen and he poured coffee into two mugs. We walked back through a long hall to a cluttered office. Arson headquarters was a collection of beaten desks set end to end with outdated computers and so many file cabinets they lined the outside halls. Galway lay down and sighed.

"How old?"

"She'll be twelve this year," he said. "She was a real worker. Now she sticks to the office."

"Good nose?"

"The best," he said. "She could lead you right to any accelerant. Now it's tough to get up these steps."

I patted the dog's head. We were kindred spirits. I'd needed a knee replacement last year. Now I'd regained the spring in my step.

"You're a persistent man," Cahill said. "You left ten messages. And then got Commissioner Foley on my ass."

I smiled and sipped my coffee. "I guess I'm not easily deterred."

"I wasn't sure what to make of it," he said. "You being a private snoop and all. But the commissioner said you were okay."

"High praise?"

"From the commissioner?" he said. "You bet. But I have to wonder, what in the hell do you think you can do that we haven't tried already? *Jesus.* This thing has been top priority. We've worked every damn angle. And when that wasn't enough, we called in ATF."

"And where did that get you?"

"Crap City."

Galway lifted her head. She scratched at something inside her ear and then lay still.

"I'm not here to critique your work," I said. "I only promised to look under a few rocks."

"Heard you might have connections?"

"Some," I said. "With bookies, leg breakers, and assorted low-lifes. The guards at Walpole and I are on a first-name basis."

"It'll take a snitch to lead us somewhere," Cahill said. "All this high-tech crap we got: photographs, video, lab results. What it'll really take is one crook turning on another. We weren't left with much. It's been tough. Tough on the department and tougher on the families. We all want to know what happened."

I nodded.

"We've ruled a lot out."

"Of course."

"And to be honest, I don't know what happened," he said. "Some people, I know, have some theories. But all that shit is just talk. I need facts."

"But there's a tape?" I said. "Or a digital image? Or whatever you have these days of someone running from the alley by Holy Innocents."

Cahill sighed and studied me. He was silent for a moment and reached for his coffee mug. Galway was in a gentle snooze, so comfortable she began to snore. Her rib cage expanded and fell with each breath. It had started to rain, a gentle patter on the windows. Thunder broke outside.

"I'd like to see it."

"Where'd you hear about it?"

"A little bird flew in my office," I said.

"Jack McGee is a big fucking bird."

I shrugged. "You and I both know I work for Jack McGee," I said. "But I do have other sources."

"Commissioner didn't want that out," he said. "I don't like it, either."

"It didn't come from Jack," I said. "And I don't work for *The Globe*. But a pair of fresh eyes on an old case never hurts."

Cahill sipped some coffee. I sipped some coffee. The rain fell and Galway snored. She had a vigorous snore. He said, "The investigation is ongoing."

"As it should be."

"Any details stay within this fucking building," he said.

"You bet."

"If news was to get out—" he said. "With all the shit we been dealing with. You might have seen we've been pretty damn busy."

"I understand. When I worked for the Middlesex DA, I learned to keep things to myself."

I asked for some more coffee and Cahill stood and left the room. It was not only a stalling technique but also because I wanted more coffee. I patted Galway's flank, thinking of Pearl aging, and waited until Cahill returned. "Do I have your word?" he said.

I nodded.

"Nobody," he said. "I mean fucking nobody is supposed to know about this."

"Sure."

He reached for his phone, dialed up somebody, and told them to come into the room.

"How good is the image?" I said.

"Terrible."

"How terrible?"

"It's nothing but a freakin' shadow," he said. "What the hell can we do with that?"

An investigator by the name of Cappelletti leaned over his desk and scrolled through dozens of video thumbnails on his laptop. Cahill had walked me down the hall and introduced us. Cappelletti, who worked as unit photographer, seemed dubious about my intentions. He had buzzed brown hair and wore a red T-shirt with jeans. He kept sunglasses on a loop around his neck and chewed gum.

"You any relation to Gino?" I said.

"Who's that?"

"Mr. Patriot?" I said.

"What'd I tell you?" Cahill said. "This generation doesn't speak our language."

The tech looked like he might have been all of fifteen. His T-shirt read ARSON. I wondered if I might print a few XLs reading GUMSHOE. I could sell them on my website if I only had one. Cappelletti kept on scrolling until he came to the frame he liked and clicked on the box.

Outside, the rain fell along Mass Ave. Cars passed with their headlamps on and windshield wipers working. A white pickup with a battered back end pulled in beside C & L Auto Body. As the truck turned, I noted C & L had their work cut out for them, as the side door had been broadsided.

"This is twenty minutes before the first call," Cappelletti said.

"Where'd you pull the video?" I said.

"Apartment building across the street," he said. "I watched it ten times before I spotted the guy. Hold on. You'll see it."

I bent down, rested my right hand on the desk, watched and waited. Cahill leaned against the office door like a bouncer, arms crossed over his big chest. Galway had stayed in his office, still snoozing.

The video showed a grainy view of Shawmut Street and several cars parked along the sidewalk. Holy Innocents was a dark old hulk, recognizable only by its heavy front doors. The counter read 19:42 and clicked off the seconds.

"You see him?" Cappelletti said.

"Him?" I said. "I only see cars."

"Behind those cars across the street," he said, pointing at the screen with a pencil. "He comes out of the church fast and then turns on Shawmut, heading south. Right at this spot. Hold on. Hold on. I'll back it up."

He used his mouse and clicked back the counter. "Five seconds from here."

Cappelletti was good. It was a bit like spotting a mosquito in a sandstorm. But at one point, a dark shadow did in fact high-step down the dark alley. He paused the image and zoomed in. He lightened the image and pointed at it again with the tip of his pencil. It appeared to be a white male wearing a ball cap and dark clothes. With the pixelation and lack of light, it may have very well been Tom Brady deflating his balls.

Cappelletti clicked the mouse and motion started again. The shadow hit the sidewalk in a sprint and ran out of the frame.

"Like I said," Cahill said from the door. "Crap City."

"What's the time before we see smoke?"

Cappelletti scrolled the video ahead several minutes. "Twelve-point-three minutes."

"We would have released it if you could see the guy's freakin' face," Cahill said. "But without more, we didn't want the guy looking over his shoulder. We want him shooting off his mouth."

"Sure," I said. "How about the vehicles parked along the curb?"

"All accounted for," Cahill said. "Christ, you think this is amateur hour?"

"Witnesses?"

"Fourteen," Cappelletti said. "Not counting responders. Spent two weeks knocking on doors in that neighborhood. It ain't the best in the South End."

"And?" I said.

"Nobody knows nothing," Cahill said. "How about you? You got anything you'd like to share with the group?"

He and Cappelletti stared at me, waiting. Cappelletti blew a bubble until it popped. I shrugged. "The building was in the process of being sold."

"Yeah," Cahill said. "Herbie Wu. So what? You think he torched it? Because that's not how things are done this century. He wouldn't have gotten half back from the insurance."

"Maybe someone didn't like him moving into the neighborhood?"

"From Chinatown?" Cappelletti said. "Pretty diverse neighborhood."

"Maybe someone leaned on him to do business so close to Southie."

"Did he pay?"

I didn't want to sell out Wu. But I shook my head.

"And who did the asking?" Cahill said.

"Working on the details," I said. "It may be nothing."

"Don't screw us, Spenser," Cahill said. "I wasn't real thrilled with you coming down here. If you know someone was leaning on Herbie Wu—"

"Would be better if we could ID the man in the alley."

Cahill and Cappelletti looked at each other. Cahill said, "And you're working on the other thing?"

I nodded.

"Who?"

"Working with the League of Unextraordinary Gentlemen," I said. "You'll be the first to know."

"Jesus Christ," Cahill said.

"I did want to ask you about this and its possible connection to all the new fires," I said. "I am a subscriber to *The Globe*. You guys have a bug."

Neither of the men spoke. Cappelletti shut the laptop.

"It's possible all of this is connected," I said. "Right?"

"You and Jack McGee."

"Busted flat in Baton Rouge," I said. "Waiting for a train."

"What the hell's he talkin' about?" Cappelletti said.

"I'd like to see the addresses and owners of all the new fires you believe are arson," I said. "Maybe I can spot a pattern."

"Right now, we have a real problem. But there's no reason to believe they're connected to Holy Innocents. We're talking about someone with a cracked head, not a professional criminal. But if you want to read this shit till you're cross-eyed, be my guest."

Galway trotted up and I patted her on the head. "I think this is the beginning of a beautiful relationship."

"Me or the dog?" Cahill said.

I simply smiled. Cahill just looked at me and shook his head before showing me the way out. As we walked down the steps, he said, "Me, Dougherty, and McGee were at the fire academy at the same time. We did three years together on Engine Thirty-three. I drove his wife home after the wake. She was so medicated, she didn't know what planet she was on. Kids still can't make sense of it."

"I'd like to help."

"Whatever it takes," he said. "I haven't slept in a long while."

Johnny ran away from a couple of condemned triple-deckers on Dot Ave with a big shit-eating grin on his face. Kevin was driving his Crown Vic that night, windows down and headlights off. He'd parked around the corner and listened to the scanner on low. Johnny opened the passenger side and slammed the big door. He was laughing. The night was hot, and Johnny's face shone with sweat.

"This one's gonna be a pissah," he said. "You see those old shingles on the roof?"

"Yeah?"

"They turn pink from wear," he said. "They're made out of gasoline. Those two buildings will burn like crazy. You'll see this thing for miles."

"You sure no one's inside?"

"Does it fucking look like anyone would live in that shithole?" he said. "Or you afraid we're going to burn up some rats? Don't be getting soft on me."

"I just thought we were going to burn that building on E Street. You know, that old warehouse?"

"We are," Johnny said. "But we burn this and it'll tie up a couple engine companies. That way we can set up shop and work on that building. We don't and they'll put it out before it really gets going."

"I don't know," Kevin said. "They can't handle all this."

"If it's not a mess, then we ain't doing any good."

"I don't know."

"You don't know dick," Johnny said. "Just drive. Everything's all set. Me and Ray already stacked some tires by the wall. He said it's covered in scrap wood and oil drums. It's all ready to go."

"Do we wait for the call on Dot Ave?"

"You worried it won't burn or somethin'?" Johnny said. "Christ."

They drove through Dorchester and up into Southie. The scanner crackled to life: Engine 21, Ladder 17, and Ladder 7. Multiple calls for a fire at 848 Dorchester Avenue. Box 7252 is being transmitted.

Kevin drove. Johnny smiled, hot wind blowing through the open windows. "What'd I fuckin' tell you?"

Johnny wore rose-tinted sunglasses that night. They were prescription, the kind that reacted to light. When he'd light up La Bomba, they'd change his eyes. He reached into the front pocket of his security guard uniform and pulled out a cigarette. He smoked it while Kevin followed the streets over to an endless warehouse on E Street. Almost all of it looked to be corrugated tin, and Kevin wondered how the hell they'd light up this beast.

Kevin had already sweated through his T-shirt. He reached for the hem and wiped his face. Driving with one hand, he slowed the Crown Vic and parked in an alley. Johnny already had La Bomba in his lap, cigarette dangling from his lips. "Here. You get the freakin' honor."

Kevin grabbed the paper bag and got out of the car. He walked to the west side of the building, close to Fargo. He found the wall Johnny had told him about, wood with tar paper and a pile of tires stacked eight feet high. All he had to do was light the match, get in the car, and roll on back to the first houses on Dot Ave. After all, if they didn't show up at a fire, some of the Sparks would start to wonder.

Kevin's heart raced and his hands shook as he set the bag next to the tire and struck the match. He got the cigarette going and ran back to the car. Two fires tonight. Johnny said they needed to do five or more tonight or it wasn't worth squat. Really get the whole department hoppin'. From Southie to Charlestown and maybe over to Brighton. It would be beautiful, he said.

Soon they were headed back to Dot Ave, seeing flames and smelling the smoke from the triple-deckers. The scanner told them it was a working fire now. The chief had called for a second and third alarm by the time they parked a few blocks away. A ton of chatter on the scanner.

At the scene, Kevin and Johnny walked through the dozen or so Sparks watching the blaze and taking pictures. Kevin raised his hand over his eyes, seeing the two buildings burning hot and bright as promised. But also seeing a third house and an apartment building starting to smoke. It had spread. The buildings were too damn close.

Johnny saw it but didn't seem to give a shit, talking with two jakes who'd just come out of the building sucking on oxygen. Johnny made some kind of joke and gave the boys a thumbs-up before walking away.

They stood around for the next half-hour before Kevin drove Johnny back to his own car. He'd left the red sedan parked inside a chain-link fence. The fence surrounding the little plot where he'd parked his security company trailer. The two sat there in the car, Johnny's pit bull going nuts by the gate.

"You see them families?" Kevin said. "We should've been more careful. This was supposed to be political."

"It is political," Johnny said. "Everything is political."

"But burning out families?" he said. "I saw ten people sitting on the curb. That old man sucking on oxygen. I don't like how this went."

"People have been hurt," Johnny said. "More will have to get hurt for someone to do something."

"Nobody's gotten hurt," Kevin said. "What the hell are you talking about?"

"Nothing."

"What?"

"Good night," Johnny said. He got out and slammed the door.

Kevin sat there for a moment, listening to the dog bark over and over. When he began to start the car, he felt a hand on his wrist. He felt like his heart might leave his chest. It was Johnny, laughing at making him jump. "You know the best part?"

Kevin shook his head.

"Those jakes back there," he said. "They thanked me. Thanked me for all the support. You know how that fucking made me feel? It's all gonna be worth it. You'll see."

After visiting the boys in Arson, I cracked my office windows that afternoon to the pleasant sound and smell of rain falling, and began to check messages. According to my service, I had eight calls from Cedar Junction, or as it's more traditionally known, MCI Walpole.

Tommy the Torch had fine timing. I returned the call.

Prisoners don't set their own hours, and I had time to walk down to Berkeley Street to buy a sub sandwich and chips. I made coffee and responded to a few e-mails. I ate most of the sub and cleaned off my desk. I paid a few bills. I checked the time. And then I called Susan. "Dr. Kildare here," I said. "I'm calling to schedule in a sponge bath after a two o'clock lobotomy."

"Are you performing your own?"

"You know ol' Dr. Gillespie," I said. "He's pretty rough on me."

"Do you have any references from after the war?"

"What can I say? I was born into the wrong era."

I swung around and faced Berkeley. The young woman in the Houghton Mifflin Harcourt building was eating lunch at her desk, too. I offered a friendly wave in solidarity. This time she waved back.

"You better watch out," I said. "Other women might appreciate my arcane references."

"I doubt it."

"Or my ability to produce a pizza later tonight."

"Pizza sounds wonderful," she said. "It's been a hell of a day for shrinkage."

"With peppers, onions, and black olives?"

She agreed and I hung up. I finished the last bit of the sub sandwich and poured some coffee. I sat at my desk and watched the rain fall for a long while.

At a quarter to five, Tommy Torch called. Actually, it was an automated voice who informed me I had a call from Cedar Junction and would I accept the charges.

"Gladly," I said.

The automated voice didn't understand. It asked me again.

"Yes," I said.

Tommy was animated, talking fast but low into the mouthpiece. He informed me that if someone learned we spoke, that the gentleman might fashion his nuts into a keychain.

"Colorful," I said.

"You unnerstand?"

"Nuts into a keychain," I said. "That's bad, right?"

"The guy we spoke of."

"Jackie DeMarco."

"For Christ sake."

"They can hear you, but not me."

"Yeah, him," he said. "He may be using this guy from up in Lynn but works in Revere. He's one of those young hotshots. A shooter. But I hear he's been branching out into other lines of work."

"Diversification."

"Yeah," Tommy said. "Right. He's also real good at burning shit. Not as good as me. But gets the job done."

"What makes you think he works for DeMarco?"

"You don't need to concern yourself with that shit, Spenser," he said. "I give you a name. If the name pans out, then you put in a good word. That's how the world works, right?"

"True pals."

"Sure," he said. "Whatever you say."

The connection from Walpole was very bad and the line buzzed in my ear. Between the rain outside my window and the mumble mouth of Tommy, it was difficult to hear. "And?"

"What?"

"The name?"

"Don't fuck me," he said.

"You needn't be concerned."

"You know Teddy Cahill?" he said. "Works in Arson?"

"And his dog, too."

"That fucking dog once got me four years inside," he said. "It's still alive? Christ."

"I'll talk to Cahill," I said. "I'll let him know if you helped. What they do is up to them."

"Okay," he said. "What the hell?"

I waited. I almost started to work out a drumroll on my desk. Instead I started to whistle the theme to *Jeopardy!*

"Tyler King," he said. Voice lowered. "A real scumbag. He's the kind of guy who'd throw acid in his mother's face. A goddamn yellow prick."

"Coming from you, a true compliment."

"Mainly does business out of his garage in Eastie," he said. "Right by Logan. Planes right overhead and shit. He's got a party store in Saugus, too. Deals drugs. But does the hard stuff that's got to be done. He ain't a nice man."

"Neither are you, Tommy," I said.

"I know what I am," he said. "If I ever forget, I got guards to remind me. I just got to know, are we good with this?"

"I guess we'll find out," I said and hung up the phone.

I grabbed my Braves cap off the hat tree and locked up the door. I called Quirk as I drove south to police headquarters. I needed information and maybe a mug shot on Tyler King.

"Why they don't make bubblegum cards for criminals?"

"Great idea," Quirk said. "I'll talk to the super. We'll get right on it, Spenser."

W hy the hell are you asking about Tyler King?" Quirk said.
"Nice choice of locations," I said. "Am I not welcome
in the new office?"

We sat in Quirk's car in the parking lot of a Burger King on
Malcolm X Boulevard.

"People will start to talk," he said. "With the new title comes
a lot of politics. I don't need that shit."

"Fair enough."

He handed me a legal-sized envelope that included two arrest
reports and three booking photos. "We liked him for two mur-
ders last year," Quirk said. "But we couldn't make it stick. You
know he's the top guy for your buddy Jackie DeMarco?"

"So I've heard."

"This shit never changes," Quirk said. "People get older. People die. New thugs take their place."

"What keeps us in business."

"His mother was a head case," Quirk said. "Dope addict. Broz had her killed and left her down in the Fort Point Channel. Funny how this all comes full circle."

"What was the murder?"

"One of the Columbia Point Dawgs was making trouble for DeMarco's growing business," Quirk said. "We found him in the trunk of an old Buick LaSalle parked in a lot at the Franklin Park Zoo."

"How old?"

"He's twenty-four," Quirk said. "When I was twenty-four, I was already married, had a kid and a mortgage. This kid's probably already killed a half-dozen people and spends what he's got on dope and broads."

"The rest he spends foolishly."

"Tyler King is no George Raft," Quirk said. "Wears his pants hanging off his ass and ball cap with a flat brim. I hear he's good with trucks. Works with his old man at a shop by Logan. He does some fleet work with trucks. Believe it or not, he's got a high IQ. I got his juvie records."

I read through the report of the gentleman who was a member of the Columbia Point Dawgs. I had read recently that entire organization was snatched up in a Federal raid and asked Quirk about it.

"Oh, yeah," he said. "Boston is now free of crime. Yippee."

"I bet you make one hell of a public speaker on career day."

"Damn right I do," Quirk said. "I tell the kids to stay off the streets or I'll bust their ass."

"I bet the teenyboppers adore you."

"Teenyboppers, hell," Quirk said. "That's what I say to kindergartners. I guess Tyler King was sick that day."

I read more and then put the reports back in the envelope.

"Keep 'em," he said. "That pic is suitable for framing."

I held it up to the light. Tyler King was not an attractive young man. He had pasty white skin, a stubbly black beard, and the long, thin face of a dope addict with short, unkempt hair. He didn't look tough. Only mean.

"You like him for torching that church?" Quirk said.

"Perhaps."

"Good source?"

"Not someone you'd want on the stand," I said.

"Your people, Spenser."

I nodded. The rain fell pleasantly in the Burger King parking lot. Smoke puffed from the little chimney that created that great charbroiled taste.

"DeMarco won't miss the next time," Quirk said.

"No," I said. "He won't."

Quirk took in a long breath and let it out slowly. His unmarked unit had that new-car smell. "But if he had anything to do with how those firefighters died, you better come straight to me or Frank."

I nodded.

"Don't pussyfoot around," Quirk said. "I don't want DeMarco to have time to take you out."

"You really do care, Marty," I said. "I'm touched."

"Now get the fuck outta my car before someone sees us together," he said.

21

An apartment was never lonely with a hot pizza, cold beer, and a lovely companion. The rain continued to patter against my bow window over Marlborough as Susan took the pizza box from my hands. I'd stopped by Pizzeria Regina in the North End on my way home. Pearl tracked the pepperoni while Susan walked to the kitchen counter.

"Hots only on my half," I said.

"The ruin of a perfectly good pizza."

"Have you ever even tried the hots?"

"And never will," she said. "I've never tried anchovies, either."

"And to think your people eat cold salmon for breakfast."

Susan shrugged and set out two plates from my good china. Actually, it was my only china.

"A captain in the Arson unit finally agreed to meet with me

today," I said. "He showed me a security video of someone, or something, leaving the scene of the fire."

"What exactly did you see?"

"A very-fast-moving shadow," I said. "I think it was a man. But that's about all I know."

"There were three fires over the weekend," Susan said. "Several families lost everything. The ones I saw on the news were Vietnamese and didn't speak English. Do they think it's the same person?"

"Arson admitted they had a problem," I said. "But when I tried to link the church fire and the recent spate, my persistence annoyed him."

"You do have a gift."

"Of persistence?"

"Of annoyance."

"Ah."

I walked to the refrigerator and fetched a cold Lagunitas. I cracked open the top and sat back at the table. Susan crossed her long, shapely legs and worked on the pizza. She had on her after-work lounging-around clothes: a soft, thin V-neck T-shirt that cost more than my shoes and khaki shorts. I appreciated the muscularity of her legs as she walked over to the couch.

"So what can you do now?" Susan said. "Hang the bad guys by their ankles?"

"Always effective," I said. "Or find a snitch who needs a favor."

"Why you were at Walpole."

"And it's such a lovely drive," I said.

I smiled and reached for more pizza. The hots really added

the proper punch to the pie. Susan Silverman had great taste in many things, but not in pizza toppings.

"Well, did your snitch do some snitching?" she said.

"I have something," I said. "A name."

"Anyone we know?"

"I hope not," I said. "This guy is a paid killer."

"What else do you know about him?"

"That in his spare time from committing murder, he enjoys setting fires," I said. "My snitch referred to him as a 'yellow prick.'"

"Illustrative."

"Coming from this guy, it was a compliment."

From my bow window, I had a decent view of the Public Garden and people walking in the rain. I broke a piece of crust from my pizza and tossed it to Pearl. She caught it in midair.

"Do you think this upstanding individual will speak to you?"

"Not a chance."

"Do you think you'll observe him in the commission of lighting a fire?"

"Nope."

"So what's the plan?" Susan said.

"When in doubt, bug the crap out of someone until they trip up," I said. "Spenser's investigation technique number eleven."

Susan nodded. "Maybe you should write a textbook?" she said.

"I thought about it," I said. "But I don't want to give up my trade secrets so easily."

"You've given them up to Z," she said.

"That's different," I said. I worked on the back half of the pizza slice. "He's my apprentice."

"Or is he Hawk's?"

"Aha," I said. "Yet to be determined."

"Have you ever considered the fact that Sixkill may be both?" Susan said. "Taking parts of each of you that will be helpful."

"That's worrisome."

"For whom?"

I thought as I chewed. I drank some beer and swallowed. "Most of the West Coast."

Susan sighed while I reached for a second slice. "I don't think it's stopped raining all day."

"Nope," I said.

"Good night to stay in."

I smiled. "If only we could think of something to do."

King's Auto Repair was on Route 1-A, a stone's throw from the Chelsea Bridge. It was in a neighborhood of breathtaking real estate, if you liked jumbo oil tanks and car impound lots. At daybreak, I parked across the street at a twenty-four-hour gym. I'd brought a couple corn muffins and coffee. I made slow work of both for the next three hours as I watched Tyler and his old man move cars from an overflow lot into four bay doors.

I assumed it was his old man. He had long gray hair and was stoop-shouldered, and was wearing blue coveralls.

Tyler didn't wear a uniform, only baggy jeans and a dirty white T-shirt. He had on a green, flat-crowned Sox cap over his greasy hair. He was rangy, with a pockmarked face and a tattoo of some sort on the back of his neck. Even with the Canon zoom, it was hard to tell what the tattoo said. Perhaps it was a smiley face reading HAVE A NICE DAY. Or GIVE PEACE A CHANCE.

At noon, I drove down 1-A toward Revere, parked along the beach, and did a hundred push-ups and sit-ups. After I got my blood flowing, I doubled back and parked one block from King's at a convenience store. I sat there for another three hours. I listened to Ella Fitzgerald sing her way through the Johnny Mercer songbook, checked messages, and watched Tyler and his dear old dad change tires.

At one point, I mentally cataloged the great fighters from Massachusetts. I started with Marvin Hagler, Rocky Marciano, and worked my way back in time to John L. Sullivan. I had not forgotten Willie Pep. If I'd started with the best, I might've started with Pep.

At almost four, Tyler King got in a black Toyota Celica, wheeled out on 1-A, and U-turned south. I started the Explorer and followed. He veered off onto Bremen Street, past several triple-deckers with billboards on their roofs, gas stations, and more garages, and stopped off at a white-brick building surrounded by concertina wire. Planes buzzed the neighborhood, shaking my windows. A sign read PAUL'S AIRPORT PARKING.

It didn't appear as though anyone but Paul had used it since the mid-1970s. Tall weeds grew from many cracks. After about five minutes, King got back into his car and headed south, rejoining 1-A.

Before we hit the tollbooth to the Sumner Tunnel, I spotted a black SUV make an inelegant turn off Porter Street and duck in two cars behind me. I kept the car in my rearview as we dipped into the tunnel. Tyler sped ahead as I hung back, keeping the SUV in my rearview mirror. I dallied a bit and the SUV made no attempt to pass. Halfway through the tunnel, the driver was only a few car lengths back.

At the tunnel exit, traffic slowed and I caught up with Tyler and the Celica by Haymarket Station. He turned left onto Congress and again onto North Street, where he drove up into a parking garage near Faneuil Hall. I kept on driving into the North End. The black SUV followed.

I picked up my phone and called the Harbor Health Club. Within two minutes, I doubled back onto Hanover and was on the phone with Hawk. I rattled off a few details.

I was back on Union and then back on North, passing the parking deck where Tyler had disappeared. At Blackstone Street, the Greenway Market was in full force. I parked along the street and joined a jumble of shoppers carrying seafood and local produce. The stalls were filled with bins of fish and oysters on ice, spinach, and carrots.

As I checked on the price of haddock, I noted two thick-necked men tailing me. Bunches of asparagus were two for five bucks. The red peppers were huge and smelled the way peppers should smell. There were onions and zucchini and more *fruits de mer*.

Under a white tent, I stopped to ask about today's scallops. The men kept walking my way.

On the Greenway, a carousel turned to calliope music. The two men approached me. They tried to act like they were shopping, but they were as unobtrusive as a couple of linebackers at a Céline Dion concert.

One of the men was built like a Bulgarian powerlifter. He

had an abnormally thick bald head and a closely trimmed black beard. He wore a navy pin-striped suit with a light blue silk shirt. The suit had to be tailored because off-the-rack would have been impossible. The other wore jeans and a white T-shirt with a mustache-goatee combo and two earrings in his left ear.

He had mean, sleepy eyes and wore a long black jacket on this particularly hot day. He looked at the powerlifter and nodded.

T hey braced me as I attempted to turn down Blackstone.

"Forget about King," Mean Eyes said. He spoke through gritted teeth. "Or we'll fuck you up bad."

I turned to him. "Is it possible to get fucked up good?"

I noted the powerlifter's head was the exact same size as some of the round watermelons at the market. Although he looked like he could bench-press a Mercedes, his communication skills were lacking. He grunted an affirmation.

The carousel turned. Children played. The calliope piped.

I preferred not to make a scene in public. But now that Tyler King was on to me, I thought we might have a chat. The two men blocked the way back to the parking garage.

"How is it, working for Jackie?" I said. "Does he provide dental?"

The guy with mean, sleepy eyes smiled. Many teeth were yellow. The others were gold.

"Guess not."

"Buzz off."

"I'm sure Killer Kowalski can try to clean and jerk me over to the Navy Yard," I said. "But here isn't the place."

Mean Eyes stepped to me and grabbed my arm. I punched him right in his bad dental work, causing his head to snap back, and he faltered a bit. Killer Kowalski stepped forward and wrapped my body in a bear hug. His strength was substantial. A short Hispanic man ran in front of his scallops and oysters in an effort to protect them.

Shoppers stepped back as Mean Eyes charged me. I leaned in to Kowalski and kicked Mean Eyes onto his backside. Kowalski hugged tighter, and it became difficult to breathe.

I rocked my head back into his face several times. His grip loosened and I slipped free. Mean Eyes reached into his coat and I kicked him in the stomach, scattering his gun across the sidewalk. A pile of aluminum tubes lay in a neat pile by the tent. I picked one up and held it like Big Papi, moving toward Killer Kowalski. The wittiest thing I could think of was "Okay, let's go."

He smiled and stepped forward. I swung and hit him in the neck. I swung again and connected with his head. The tube made a hollow musical sound as it connected with bone. Killer was unfazed. He had dark skin and black eyes. With the tailored suit and big gold watch, he had the appearance of a pro athlete. His muscles swelled in the tailored suit.

I stepped forward, fist raised.

To my amazement, he did the same, and we began to circle each other like a couple of stray dogs.

People were screaming now. Someone was yelling for the cops. Blood rushed into my ears and my vision narrowed. My body felt light and loose and I wanted to hit the man again and again. Mean Eyes jumped on my back and I turned backward and ran him into the big table of shellfish. The table broke; ice and shellfish scattered. The Hispanic owner yelled that he was calling the cops, too.

I got back on my feet.

People in the market scattered as we fought. I searched for the aluminum pole but could not find it. I tasted blood in my mouth as I stepped forward. He was a few inches taller than me and about the girth of an American brown bear. If I got close to his body, he'd get me to the ground. Never let a bear get the upper hand.

I stepped forward, throwing a right, and he ducked it. He came up with a right and connected. I saw stars popping and stepped back. My breathing was very good. My newly reconstructed knee worked great. He was no more to me than just a thick heavy bag. I stepped in with a combination on his body. My blows were fast and hard but seemed to show no effect on him. He countered with a barrage that brought tears to my eyes.

I stepped back, fists raised. I threw a right and a hook. The hook connected. He nodded in appreciation. His eye began to bleed. The man almost seemed to enjoy it.

It was only us. Wind rushed down Blackstone Street, fluttering the tents. I heard sirens way off. I landed a hard right. He landed two quick jabs in my ribs. They hurt a great deal.

Just as it was about to get interesting, Mean Eyes stepped in with a gun. Killer tried to wave him off. The man wanted more.

Hawk entered the alley. Both men looked to him. And then at each other. They turned, but not before Killer wiped the blood from his busted eye and nodded. I attempted to catch my breath as they turned and walked away with purpose.

"Who the hell was that?" I said.

"New blood," Hawk said.

There were sirens coming close. The Hispanic man was calling me unpleasant names in Spanish. Hawk grabbed my elbow and turned me away from the market and out of the alley.

24

My hand was in a bucket of ice.

Tyler King was seated in a chair before me. I'd already assaulted two men in a very public place. Why not add kidnapping to the mix? Z had insisted Tyler join us after he'd made a drop of some kind at the Quincy Market. Z had a small bruise under one eye. King had several more. Hawk leaned against a concrete wall and waited by a metal door.

We were in a storage cellar around the corner from a bar where Z worked as a bouncer. Z wore jeans, work boots, and a black T-shirt with the sleeves cut out. It read ROCKY BOY, MONTANA ALL-STARS.

"Go fuck yourself," Tyler said.

"Witty," Hawk said.

"Who the hell are you?"

Hawk didn't move. He stood in the shadow with shades on. "Hawk," he said.

Tyler swallowed. He had dirty hands, grease under his stubby fingernails. He wore a green Sox cap like they pass out free on St. Paddy's Day. I stepped in closer and got a good look at his neck tattoo. Mickey Mouse extending his middle finger.

"What the hell?" he said. "Why're you busting my nuts? What'd I ever do to you?"

"We work for Disney," I said. "I know a lawyer there. Did you realize you're guilty of copyright infringement?"

I turned to Hawk. He started to whistle "Zip-a-Dee-Doo-Dah." *"Song of the South."*

"Yes, suh," Hawk said.

Z smiled. Hawk and I had perfected our act long ago. We were the Martin and Lewis of beating the crap out of people. My hand hurt. My ribs hurt. Jackie DeMarco had definitely traded up in his hired help.

"Who sent you?" Tyler said. "Christ. You can't stick a fucking gun in a guy's back and knock him around until he talks. This ain't some Arab country. Shit. We got rights here."

"Sure," I said. "But how about a little talk. Or else my associates here might take you out on a deep-sea fishing trip and use you as bait."

"Bullshit," Tyler said. "Hawk does shit for money. How much money do you want to let me go?"

Hawk shook his head. "This ain't for pay."

"How about you, Pancho Villa?" Tyler said, looking to Z. "I'll give you a lot of pesos."

"I'm full-blooded Cree," Z said, muscular arms crossed over his chest. "We get paid in scalps."

Tyler swallowed again and turned his eyes up to me. He looked at me and nodded and said, "What do you want?"

"I want to know why Jackie DeMarco had you burn that church in the South End."

"What the fuck?" Tyler said. He began to laugh. "I got no freakin' idea what you're talking about. He didn't burn a god-damn church."

Hawk stepped up out of the shadows and into a slice of light. Tyler looked up into the light and blinked. I held up a hand for him to wait. Hawk took a step back. There was a single bulb in the room shining on many boxes of liquor. A wino's dream.

"Jackie wanted to send a message," I said, "after he started cutting into Gino Fish's territory."

Tyler narrowed his eyes and shook his head. "Who the fuck is a Gino Fish?"

I shook my head at his lack of understanding of local history. My hand rattled around in the ice. I pulled it out and examined it. My knuckles were fat and getting fatter. I stuck it back in the bucket. My ribs ached with each breath. I figured a couple might've been cracked.

"I can hit him," Z said. "I'd like to hit him again."

Tyler winced and turned his head. Z grinned, standing tall and still.

"Why'd you have me followed?" I said.

Tyler jacked his head up at me. He stared at me and yelled, "I got no fucking idea what you're talking about."

"Two guys," I said. "Black SUV picked me up before we went into the tunnel. You called ahead after you got tipped I was coming."

Tyler snored. "Nobody tipped nobody."

"Double negative," Hawk said. "A terrible reflection of today's education system."

I held up my swelling hand and said, "We met," I said. "They told me. One of them looked like he just escaped a traveling circus."

"So fucking what?" Tyler said. He smiled, pleased that his connection to DeMarco was now public knowledge.

Z looked to Hawk. Hawk stayed by the door. Outside, you could hear the late-afternoon bustle around Faneuil Hall and the market. People yelling and hooting. Ready to party on a Friday night. Two-for-one cocktails. Guinness on tap. Jell-O shooters for everyone.

"Go ahead and scream," Z said. "Nobody gives a shit."

I looked to Z and nodded. Z walked up to Tyler King and snatched up a good bit of his shirt. Z pulled back his arm, which when coiled resembled Secretariat's hind leg.

"They were with me," Tyler said. "But nobody tipped me. I saw you over at the Muscle Factory and then over at the packie. You got a blue Explorer. I know fucking cars. It's my goddamn job."

"Nope," I said. "You got tipped. You were waiting for me."

"Believe what you want."

"All we want to know is about the fire," I said. "I know what you do for Jackie. And I know why you burned the church. You lit it in the cellar in two places and then hauled ass in that alley.

I saw you on surveillance tape. You can either talk to me about it. Or I'd be more than fine calling the police."

"Call 'em," Tyler said. "And I'll sue the fucking Mex for assault and kidnapping."

"Cree," Z said. And then he punched him once but very effectively in the face.

"I don't know nothing about no fucking church fire," Tyler said. He spit out some blood. "Mr. DeMarco wouldn't ever touch a church. Are you nuts? He goes to Mass every Sunday with his wife and kids. That's some crazy bad luck."

"It wasn't going to be a church anymore," I said. "The archdiocese had sold it. It was sold to a man named Herbie Wu."

"Am I not speaking English?" Tyler said. "I got no fucking idea. How many ways can I say it?"

"Then tell DeMarco I want to talk," I said. "You set the fire. But he called it."

"Jesus Christ, man," Tyler said. "You can beat the crap out of me. Toss me in the ocean. Do what you want. But that doesn't change that we didn't burn no fucking church. Now either let's get down to the beatin' or let me fucking go."

No one spoke for a good thirty seconds. My hand swelled with each breath. The storage room was small and tight. I felt empty and hollow after the adrenaline surge of the fight. I looked down to Tyler and his small, hard eyes.

"Let him go."

Z didn't seem pleased. But Hawk held open the door. Light poured into the dark room and Tyler stumbled to his feet.

"Jackie won't like this," Tyler said. "Jackie ain't gonna forget this one goddamn bit."

After he left, Hawk closed the door. We gathered like bugs under the single warehouse light. Hawk shook his head. "Mmm."

"You believe him," I said. "Don't you?"

Hawk nodded.

I looked up to Z. He shrugged in agreement. "Now what?"

"Wait for the best-laid plans to unravel."

"Or Jackie DeMarco to shoot your ass," Hawk said.

"Yes," I said. "Or that."

Rob Featherstone was a Spark. He'd been a Spark for maybe twenty years, running the fire museum and handing out coffee when he wasn't playing with his model trains. He was a tall bald guy, with what hair he had left dyed jet black on his freckled head. "My back," he'd say. "If I hadn't screwed up my back, I'd been a Boston firefighter. All I ever wanted since I was a kid in Brockton."

Featherstone had cornered Kevin at the Scandinavian, right as he was about to hang it up for the night. Two more fires, this time set by Johnny and Big Ray. Kevin had followed the fires, gone back for a cup of black coffee before getting home. He had an early day of work at the Home Depot.

"He's freakin' nuts," Featherstone said. "Crazy as a

shithouse rat. I don't want to say nothin' bad about him. I just want you to know who you're dealing with."

"Who?"

"Who the hell you think?" he said. "Fucking Johnny Donovan. You're a young guy. Impressionable. What are you, twenty-one? Hadn't you taken the fire exam?"

"Twice."

"Yeah," Featherstone said. "And maybe next time you'll pass, you know? You don't want Johnny Donovan anywhere around you. He's bad, bad news. Tried to join up with us five years ago and we wouldn't have him. The way he rides around in that red Chevy, misrepresenting himself as a real-life jake. I mean, come on. He's like a crazy uncle I once had who thought he was Napoleon. Wore military outfits and the whole deal before they sent him off to Bridgewater."

"Don't worry about me."

"He's got the crazy eyes, Kevin," he said. "I've seen it. And that fucking guy Ray. I know he's a cop, but the department up there has no use for him. They been wanting to shit-can him for four years. He knows he doesn't have much time. It just pains me, seeing you sitting there with those two. Bad news."

"Okay." Kevin got up to leave. "Thanks."

Featherstone held up a hand. "Wait," he said. "There's more. I want to ask you something."

Kevin waited.

"Has either one of those two talked to you about all these fires?"

Kevin took a breath. He started to sweat. But kept it cool, breaking off a piece of donut and shrugging. "Not really. Why?"

"Something happened the other night," Featherstone said. "At that triple-decker fire. Something that got me thinking."

Kevin studied the man's face and the ink-black hair sticking out from the side of his head. "I don't know," Featherstone said. "As soon as that fire started, there was another one. On Dot Ave. At an old warehouse. You know?"

"I heard something about it."

"Two set off back to back," Featherstone said. "Just got me thinking, is all."

"Thinking about what?"

Featherstone leaned back in the booth. He shrugged and rubbed the top of his bald head before leaning in and saying, "I saw Johnny's red car at that warehouse the night before. I didn't think much of it. Isn't he in security or some shit?"

"Yeah," Kevin said. "He's got a lot of contracts to watch old buildings. It's what he does."

"Just doesn't set right with me, is all," Featherstone said. "Him being crazy and then seeing his car. I just wanted to warn you before I tip the boys."

"The boys?"

"Arson," Featherstone said. "They should talk to him. Even if he didn't have nothing to do with it, he'd know something about the building."

Kevin felt his breath catch in his throat. He stopped chewing his donut.

"Just stay clear, buddy boy," Featherstone said, sliding out. "Don't get the shit splattered on you."

Kevin nodded and smiled. Featherstone left the pastry shop, a low buzzing of fluorescent lights overhead. He looked to the cash register to make sure the woman working there was in back. He picked up the phone and called Johnny Donovan. It was nearly two a.m.

He picked up on the first ring.

"What?"

"We got some trouble."

The cops came for me the next morning. Thankfully, I'd just changed into a fresh T-shirt and jeans, replacing a butterfly bandage on my right eye. Feeling fine and somewhat dandy, I walked down my steps onto Marlborough and spotted Frank Belson leaning against a black unmarked unit. The rear door was wide open. Belson absently puffed on a cigar and waved me inside.

"And if I refuse?"

"You won't get to meet the new boss," Frank said. "And I'd really hate to miss that."

I shook my head and crawled into the backseat. Belson slammed the door, put out his cigar, and got behind the wheel. We drove off in the opposite direction of the Public Garden before he took Berkeley over to Storrow. It was past rush hour and the road had yet to become clogged. Belson followed the

Esplanade as a middle-aged woman in the passenger seat turned around to me and said, "Just what the fuck do you think you're doing, getting into a wrestling match at the farmers' market?"

"Tea Party Museum was too far of a walk."

"You can't pull crap like that anymore," she said. "Tourists took video of you with their cell phones. You're gonna be very popular on YouTube."

"Spenser, this is Captain Glass," Belson said. "She doesn't like me smoking in the car, either."

"And I don't give any free passes to aging thugs who drink beer with cops."

I met Belson's eye in the rearview mirror and raised my eyebrows. "Sometimes Frank and I drink cheap bourbon."

Glass had shoulder-length brown hair and green, unsmiling Irish eyes. Her skin was the color of milk, which contrasted with her black silk blouse. She wore a small gold cross on a lightweight gold chain around her neck and just a trace of red lipstick.

"You were easy to spot," Glass said. "But so was the other man."

"The other man who we understand attacked you," Belson said. "Right?"

"That's right, Officer," I said. "He came out of nowhere."

"However it happened," Glass said, "several vendors want to press charges against you and the other man."

"Send the bill to Jackie DeMarco," I said.

Belson turned off at Mass Ave and doubled back down Commonwealth. I took it as a good sign we weren't headed south to police headquarters. The direction meant this was a meet and greet and not an arrest. Had it been night, I might have thanked my lucky stars.

"I should feel honored they sent Homicide to pick me up," I said. "However, the last time I saw the big guy, he was still breathing."

"His name is Davey Stefanakos," Belson said. "He's got a rap sheet that looks like the *Encyclopedia Britannica*. Before he got into the life, he was in the Army and did a lot of that mixed martial arts crap."

I touched the bandage over my eye and let out a long, painful breath. "Didn't feel like crap to me."

"Get over it," Belson said. "You think you can retain the belt forever? Someone's coming up. Someone's always coming up these fucking streets."

"You'll have to deal with that crap on your own," Glass said. "We want to talk to you about a guy named Rob Featherstone."

"Sure," I said. "Remind me again. Who's Rob Featherstone?"

"The guy from the Sparks museum you talked to last week," Belson said. "And a poor unfortunate bastard. Somebody dumped his body off the Tobin Bridge last night. Some college kids farting around on sailboats fished him out of the water."

"Was he already dead?"

"Somebody was real pissed off," Belson said. "Shot twice in the back of the head. Twice in the back."

"Ouch."

"We understand you spoke with him in connection to Holy Innocents?" Glass said. "You're working for a Boston firefighter off the books."

"I can't divulge my client list," I said.

"Zip it up, Spenser," Belson said. "We're on the same team. Featherstone loved firefighting so much, he'd get up in the middle of the night and chase sirens."

"And what do you do?"

"I get paid for it," Belson said. "Featherstone did it for free. In my book, that makes you a little screwy."

"He seemed like a nice guy," I said. "What else can you say about a person who hands out coffee and donuts to men on the job?"

"Just what did he tell you?" Glass said. "Did he know anything about the church fire?"

"No," I said. "Mainly I looked at Arthur Fiedler's helmet collection."

"Yes or no, Spenser," Belson said. He stopped at a traffic light. "Yes or no."

"He talked about what he saw," I said. "But nothing he said was of any help to me. Or anything that might've gotten him killed."

"His wife said he'd become obsessed with all these summer fires," Glass said. "He nearly lost his day job hopping from place to place. He told her he'd figured out what was going on and was damn well going to do something about it."

"And who'd he suspect?"

"Well, that's the problem," Belson said. The car lurched forward on Commonwealth as we made our slow, steady way toward the Public Garden. "Never told her. Found his car down in the Seaport. Cleaned of all prints. Some blood on the window glass, which we're pretty sure is his."

"Friends?"

"Not many," Glass said. "We're working on it."

"Maybe it's a coincidence?" I said.

"Belson," Glass said. "I thought you told me this guy was smart."

"Lucky," Belson said. "I told you he was often lucky, Captain."

W here's Galway?" I said.

"In the back room playing poker with the other hounds." Teddy Cahill looked up from the bar and shrugged. "What the fuck happened to you?"

I touched the bandage on my eye. "I disturbed some local wildlife."

"Looks more like it disturbed you," Cahill said.

I took a seat next to him. It was just after six at Florian Hall, the fire union headquarters down in Dorchester. The union had an impressive array of banquet rooms, offices, and, most important, a bar. Cahill walked behind the bar, popped the top of a Sam Adams, and slid it over to me. We were the only ones in the large space.

"I always admired you guys."

"Yeah, yeah," he said.

"You know a guy named Rob Featherstone?"

"Sure," he said. "Works over at the fire museum. He's a Spark."

"Was a Spark," I said. "He's dead."

"No shit." Cahill cut his eyes over at me. "He wasn't the bastard who got dumped off the bridge?"

I nodded and drank some Sam Adams. The union knew how to calibrate their cooler. The beer was ice cold. In a separate room, a rock band was warming up for a wedding. The walls vibrated pictures of long-dead union members and guys standing among the ruins of many buildings. "A police lieutenant named Belson just braced me, thinking he might be tied to the arson case."

"Yeah, I know Frank," Cahill said. "He should've called."

"Check your messages," I said. "I'm sure he will."

"I thought it was a suicide," Cahill said. "Heard the guy jumped."

"He had an incentive," I said. "There were four bullet holes in him."

"Christ."

"Had he talked to you about the church fire?"

Cahill stubbed out the cigarette and scratched his cheek. "Nope," he said. "Not a word. Or anybody else from the Sparks, for that matter. Rob Featherstone. Really? I think he collected model trains or some shit."

The band launched into the first few bars of Foreigner's "Hot Blooded." They got to the part where the fever reached a hundred and three and stopped to make some adjustments.

"Could he have contacted someone else in Arson?" I said. "Maybe as a confidential source?"

"Sure," Cahill said. "It's possible. But I doubt it. We tend to talk amongst ourselves on stuff like that. And if a guy like Featherstone had known something, he wouldn't have kept it a secret. Those Sparks really bleed for the department. They come out at all hours looking out for us. I mean, this is a thankless job sometimes. Just like being a cop. Someone gives you a pat on the back and it's appreciated."

"Sometimes comely young women hand me a shot of rye on the street," I said. "Gumshoe boosters."

Cahill grunted under the walrus mustache.

"I interviewed Featherstone last week," I said. "He didn't offer anything. He said he got there maybe two minutes before the engines. He talked a lot about Dougherty, Bonnelli, and Mulligan. But Belson says Featherstone told his wife he knew who'd been setting all the fires the last few months. Maybe Holy Innocents."

"And?"

"And he never told her or told the police," I said.

"Of course not," he said.

"Yep."

"Son of a bitch."

Cahill hadn't touched his beer since I walked in. He opened a pack of cigarettes and pulled out a fresh one. It had been a while since I'd been around so much smoke. I figured the union didn't think the smoke would offend the firefighters. I drank some more beer. The band turned it up to eleven, rocking out to Eddie Money, "Baby Hold On."

"Jesus," Cahill said. "What is this, the summer of fucking '78?"

"You remember that far back?"

"Only when I drink."

"Busy week?"

"Eight more suspicious fires," Cahill said. He streamed smoke out of the side of his mouth. "It's what keeps me young."

"I'll check with the museum and let you know what I find out."

Cahill nodded. He looked up at the collection of booze bottles on the shelf and the dusty framed photographs of firefighters then and now. A ceramic figurine of a little boy dressed in fireman's garb stood tall by the whiskeys. He was holding a cute little ax.

"You want to be straight about what happened to your freakin' eye?"

"I was following a guy named Tyler King and some of his friends threw up a roadblock," I said. "We made a real mess out of some *fruits de mer*."

"I got a nice file on Tyler King."

"We just had a chat yesterday."

Cahill shook his head. "But he's not your guy," he said. "All these fires ain't his work, Spenser. We eliminated him a long time ago."

"'All these fires'?" I said. "Hmm. Are you coming around to the idea of one guy?"

Cahill blew out a long stream of smoke. He shook his head. "Tyler King is a pro," he said. "He does what he does for money and that's it. All these fucking fires. This is something else. It's the goddamnedest thing I've ever seen."

"Everything started at Holy Innocents?"

Cahill touched his mustache. I drank some beer in the silence. After the second sip, he stared at me and just nodded. "Okay. Okay."

"How?"

"Some of the new ones look like what we found at Holy Innocents."

"Which was what?"

"Stuff," he said. "Similar stuff."

"Hold on," I said. "Don't get too technical with me."

Cahill shrugged and reached for his beer. He drank a sip. Hot damn. We were making some progress.

He reached for some Bushmills and poured out two shots. "Commissioner would shit a golden brick if I told you this. Nobody wants the public to panic over some nutso. But by my last estimate, we've had at least eighty."

"Yikes."

"From now on I want to know what you know," he said. "And I won't hold back, either. Me and you are working together."

"In cahoots?"

"Unofficial or official, I don't give a shit," Cahill said. "But this fucking guy is burning up this town. Three of our people are dead, and I know that won't be the last of it. This guy is getting his rocks off."

"How do you know it's a guy?"

"'Cause he sends us letters," Cahill said. "Don't you let that get out. Son of a bitch calls himself Mr. Firebug. Sent all that shit over to ATF and didn't get squat."

"Mr. Firebug," I said. "Very gender-specific."

Cahill raised his eyes at me, put down the cigarette, and stroked his mustache. "Don't hold back nothing."

He slid the shot of Bushmills closer. We both reached for the shots and drank them together.

W ould you mind if I kidnapped you for the weekend?"
I said.

"What's the occasion?"

"Have you forgotten?"

"I'd sometimes like to forget my birthday," she said. "But I
figured you might with all this fire business."

"How could I forget?" I said. "You wrote it in my DayMinder."

"I don't know," Susan said. "Would a birthday kidnapping
include champagne and room service?"

"Absolutely."

"Okay," she said. She tapped at her cheek with an index finger. "I can be willingly accosted. But are you sure you can afford
taking a couple days off?"

"Don't worry," I said. "Trouble will be waiting when I return. We leave Friday. I made reservations. Pearl can stay with Henry."

"Isn't that presumptuous?"

"Presumptuous is that I'm not packing a lot of clothes."

"And what should I pack?"

"The black bikini," I said. "I've bought a few things for you from La Perla."

"They must love you there," she said.

"I buy you another getup," I said, "and they'll throw in a free pair of knickers."

Susan drummed her fingers on the table. We'd found a nice corner booth at Alden & Harlow, still finding it hard to believe the space had once been Casablanca. I'd ordered their Secret Burger and Susan asked for a bruised tomato salad. She had a glass of sauvignon blanc while I stayed on my Sam Adams kick from Florian Hall. Continuity was important.

"I like the bandage," Susan said. "It's kind of cute."

I touched my brow, having forgotten, and smiled. And then I showed her my right hand knuckles, purplish and swelling.

"Not so cute."

"A hazard of the job."

Susan took a healthy sip. Half the glass was gone.

"And the other fella?" she said.

"Sort of like punching the cab of a Mack truck."

"Yikes," Susan said. "Big?"

"I thought of him as Killer Kowalski's older and more physically developed brother."

The food arrived. The waitress, a cute young woman with

black hair and purple highlights, placed the plates before us with some flourish. She asked if we had everything we needed. I looked to Susan, gripped her hand under the table, and said, "You bet."

"And would it spoil the surprise if you told me where?"

"The Cape."

"That narrows it."

"Hyannis."

"That narrows it a bit more."

"Our old place," I said. "Where we used to go."

"The old Dunfey's?" she said.

I took a bite of the Secret Burger and nodded. The burger was spot-on.

"Aren't you nostalgic," Susan said.

"It's been more than twenty years," I said. "Back then, you were afraid of Hawk."

"*Afraid* isn't the word," she said. "More like scared shitless for you."

Her bruised tomatoes, although impressive, looked like I felt. She took a bite of the salad as I worked on the hamburger. Alden & Harlow chefs were artists. I tried to make it last. Susan laughed at me, reached over, and wiped some high-end ketchup off my chin.

"Okay," she said. "I'll let you kidnap me. But only for nostalgia's sake."

"I heard they turned our bedroom into a shrine," I said. "Holy men come there to pray. It promises to grant amazing prowess."

"It's where you—"

"Opened the heavens?"

"We'd already done that many times," Susan said. "It's where we forged our bond. In a very real sense, where we made a life-time commitment to each other."

"With only one brief and yet unimportant interruption."

"You call that time unimportant?" she said.

"No," I said. "But the other people involved were."

"We never discuss that time."

I looked up from my drink. "Would it be helpful?"

"Nope."

I offered my Sam Adams across the table. Susan lifted her wine and we touched glasses with a sharp clink.

"To the future?" she said.

"'Art is long,'" I said. "'And Time is fleeting.'"

Rob Featherstone had lived in a blue cottage, like they built for GIs after the war, a few blocks from the water in Quincy. The next morning, I stepped over several flower arrangements set on the steps and mashed the buzzer. Within a minute or two, a woman opened the door. She was in her mid-sixties, with a long, drawn face and sagging shoulders. She wore narrow glasses and a Sox hoodie over a gray shirt.

I told her I'd worked with her Rob. A solid half-lie.

She nodded, reached into the hoodie, and grabbed a tissue. She wiped her eyes, blew her nose, and said she was Mrs. Featherstone.

"I'm very sorry to hear about Rob."

She nodded and wandered back in the little house. I opened the storm door and followed. A handful of people sat in the living room with more talking back in the kitchen. Mrs. Featherstone walked back from the kitchen and nodded to a small dining room. The table was finely polished. The seats had been covered in protective plastic. On the walls hung prints of old locomotives and coal burners. Several model train engines sat side by side on the table with a track encircling the table.

"You a Spark?"

"I'm a private investigator. Rob was helping me with an arson case."

"Christ Almighty," she said. "I knew they were going to kill him."

"Who?"

"The damned arsonists," she said, wiping her nose again. Her nose was very red and her eyes completely glazed over. "Don't you know about all these crazy fires?"

"And who are they?"

She shook her head. "Hell if I know," she said. "But Rob did. He was sure of it. Just sure of it."

"Besides you, who would he confide in?"

"I don't know," she said. "Jerry Ramaglia? He's here. Other Sparks. Rob saw them more than he saw me. When he wasn't at work, he lived at that firehouse museum."

"You think he meant someone who was a Spark?"

"I don't know," she said. "He didn't tell me nothing. We'd been together for forty years. But the last thirty hadn't been so easy. We stayed together for the kids, and then the kids leave and we stay together 'cause it's easy. Even if Rob wasn't an easy man to be around. Chasing fires and playing with his model trains."

"But he told you that he knew who set all these fires."

"Yes."

"And what else?"

"That he was going to do something about it."

"And you didn't ask him what he meant?"

"To be honest, I thought it was just talk," she said. "Rob always had some kind of conspiracy theory working. I just said, 'Good luck with that, dear,' and turned the newspaper while eating toast. But they killed him. Didn't they?"

"Someone did."

"Couldn't've been anything else," she said. "Rob was an electrician. He fixed and wired shit. He did good work. Never pissed anyone off. Wasn't into getting drunk or drugs or crap like that. He loved being a Spark. It was his life."

She blew her nose long and hard. There was an odd burst of laughter from the kitchen. A man walked into the dining room and asked if we would like some coffee. We both shook our heads and the man disappeared.

"God," she said. "Someone killed him. He finally did it."

"Did what?"

"Something really important."

"You don't mean that."

"Yes, I do," she said. "I'm sad for him. 'Cause he's dead. But he finally did something big for Boston Fire. He would have loved that."

"And if he did have some big information, might he have shared it with Jerry?"

"I don't know," she said. "Better ask Jerry."

I nodded. "Did Rob keep a journal or have a personal computer?"

"He had both."

"May I see them?"

She shrugged and looked down at her hands. She twisted the tissue in her fingers. "Cops got all that," she said. "They came over and took everything last night."

I nodded again.

"But you're not with the cops."

"No."

"Boston Fire?"

"Nope."

"Who do you work for?"

"Spenser."

"And who's that?"

I pointed to myself, smiled, and again offered my condolences. She stood, walked me from the room, and pointed out Jerry Ramaglia, who was visible through a pair of French doors. Outside, I found him pacing and smoking a cigarette. He had on a ball cap that told me he was assistant chief of the Sparks Association. Soon he might need a new hat.

I asked him about Featherstone talking about the arsons.

"Nah," he said. "I never heard him say that. He knew something about who torched that church or any of those warehouses and he'd a told me. We spent pretty much every day together. We were at that fire. Worked it all night. Yeah. He knew something about an arson and he'd have called me straight off. Between you and me, the wife is a little . . . you know."

He swirled his index finger beside his head.

"Cuckoo for Cocoa Puffs?"

"Right."

"You think she made it up?"

"I didn't say that," he said. "But maybe she's not remembering things right. You know she's in shock. Maybe she's trying to make some sense of someone shooting Rob. He's just a nice guy. No one would want to kill someone like Rob Featherstone. Whoever did it just wanted his wallet. He got jacked. But not 'cause he knows something. That's really nuts."

"Did he tell you that I'd stopped by?"

"He only told me he'd met a private investigator at the museum," he said. "He told me you were looking into the fires and told me to ask around for you."

"Can you still put out the word with the Sparks?"

"Sure," he said. "Of course. Whatever it takes to find who did this to Rob."

"Did he have a computer he used at the museum?"

"Just for business," he said. "Not personal. We take inventory on it for T-shirt sales, fund-raisers, and all that."

"Security cameras?"

"Nah," he said. "But I'll talk to the boys. We're going to get together tonight at the museum. He was a good chief. A really good one. A born leader. Did he tell you that a fireman saved his life when he was a kid?"

I shook my head.

"He was on the top floor of a triple-decker and everyone got out except for him and his sister," he said. "A jake busted open his bedroom window and carried him and his sister out at the same freakin' time. He never forgot it. Felt he owed it to these guys the rest of his life."

He crushed the cigarette under the heel of his shoe. He

looked up at me. More people had arrived at the cracker-box house. Ramaglia looked in the window and then back to me. "I gotta get back to everyone."

"Of course."

"You think he really might've been on to something?" he said. "One guy doing all this shit?"

"Police are taking it seriously."

"Be a hell of a thing if we could stop all this burning. I don't think I've had a good night's sleep all freakin' summer."

"What kind of person would want to set fires every night?"

Ramaglia shrugged and took a deep breath. "Someone good and smart," he said. "He's got some sense about how it's done and how to do it. That takes some kind of genius nutso."

29

On the way home, I dropped by the Engine 8/Ladder 1 firehouse in the North End. Jack McGee and another firefighter were unloading groceries from the back of a pickup truck. I helped them carry the load up to the second floor, making a couple trips down to the pickup truck on Hanover.

"You caught me at a bad time, Spenser," Jack said. "I'm supposed to cook tonight."

"How about I help," I said. "And we talk."

"You any good?" he said. "This is a tough crew."

"Could Bobby Orr skate?"

"Go to it, chief," McGee said. "I was going to make some hamburger steaks and mashed potatoes. But you can use anything we have in the galley."

I sorted through the pantry and the commercial-size refrigerator, perused the newly arrived boxes and bags. I found several pounds of shrimp in the freezer, some white rice in the pantry, and many onions and peppers fresh from the store. I stood back, folded my arms across my chest, and nodded at McGee. "Can your boys take the spice?"

"Yeah, sure," he said. "And if they can't, the others will bust their balls."

"How many?"

"We got eight, maybe nine."

"You have six pounds of shrimp in the freezer," I said. "I can add some vegetables and rice and make shrimp étouffée."

McGee shrugged. "Sounds good to me," he said. "What else do you need?"

"A bottle of Tabasco," I said. "And a couple loaves of crusty bread."

"I'll send someone down to the Salumeria Italiana."

I nodded. "Perfect."

McGee tossed a very manly white apron to me and I wrapped it around my waist. I grabbed the shrimp and set them to thaw under running water. Placing a chopping board on the counter, I went to work on the onions, peppers, celery, and garlic. "You think they might have some green onions at the Salumeria?"

"We'll get 'em," he said. "What can I do?"

"Do you know how to make a roux?"

"What the fuck is that?"

"A Louisiana gravy."

"Nope," he said. "But I can try."

I found a black skillet the size of a wagon wheel and set it on the burner. I took several sticks of butter from the refrigerator and olive oil and flour from the cabinet. I explained how you kept the burner on medium and stirred in a stick of butter with a little oil with a half-cup of flour. "Keep stirring it until it turns the color of toffee."

"Whaddya want to talk to me about?"

"I just got back from a wake for Rob Featherstone."

"Yeah," McGee said. "I heard about Rob. He was a little odd, but a good egg, you know? He took care of me and the boys. He'd been a Spark for longer than I been a firemen."

"His wife thinks he knew something about the arsons."

McGee stopped stirring the butter. I could see it was beginning to burn and made the hand motion for him to continue. The smell of melting butter with the flour and spices wasn't too bad. I wanted to crack open a cold beer, but drinking at the firehouse was a little frowned upon.

"Okay," he said. "Are you talking Holy Innocents? Or the others?"

"Cahill admitted the church and these warehouse fires are connected."

"Son of a bitch," he said. "Finally, they admit it."

"The guy calls himself Mr. Firebug and taunts Arson with letters," I said. "The commissioner doesn't want anyone to panic or for it to get out to the media."

"The media would love that shit," McGee said. He kept dutifully stirring. "Mr. Firebug. Shit. I always felt the church was a revenge thing, but what about these warehouses and abandoned houses? What gives?"

"I would've guessed revenge, too," I said. "But for the first time in my life, it turns out I was wrong."

"The first time?"

"I know," I said. "Can you believe it?"

"Nope."

I walked up next to McGee. He was a thick-bodied guy and took up a lot of space by the stove. I examined his roux. Still not brown enough. "Keep stirring."

"Okay, okay."

I went back to chopping. Out the window, there was a nice view of Hanover Street and the Paul Revere statue. Tourists surrounded Paul and took photos with him and his horse while I made fine work of the garlic, chopped onion, green pepper, and celery.

If I'd had more time to prep, I would've made shrimp stock with the shells and heads. But the étouffée would stand on its own.

I peered back into the skillet. I scraped the onions, green peppers, and celery into a bowl. I dumped the bowl into the skillet and told McGee to keep it going.

"Cahill must have some physical evidence he's sitting on," McGee said. "Right?"

"Between me, you, and the étouffée?" I said. "He has some fragments of some type of device. Same stuff has shown up at some recent fires."

"And now Rob Featherstone is dead," he said. His big face shone with sweat while he worked. "You know, we had a fire three days ago on Endicott, near the Greenway. We thought it was an abandoned building but found some guy on the second floor with his damn dog. He'd been sleeping and saw the smoke, but he was afraid to leave. We got him out and had to get up on the roof to put out the third floor."

"More people are going to get hurt."

"I'm just saying we get at least one or two of these a week," McGee said. "You know how many we used to work?"

I shook my head.

"Maybe one like this every six months."

"You gotta hate prolific psychopaths," I said. "Mr. Firebug."

"Any fucking guy calling himself that should get his nuts handed to him."

"Keep stirring," I said. "Don't burn the roux."

"I don't even know what I'm doing here."

"Me and you both, McGee."

Z and I jogged along the Charles River on a route I knew so well I could run it backward with my eyes closed. I had already packed for the Cape and would pick up Susan in Cambridge after her last appointment. The investigation could wait until Sunday. We ran three miles at a fast clip, sprinting at every mile marker and then a full-out race at the end toward the Hatch Shell.

As Z was quite a bit younger than me, I let him win. No reason to embarrass him.

We cooled down with a half-mile walk. We both moved with our hands laced above our heads. It was early, but the morning sun had already started to bake the sidewalk. The Esplanade was busy with runners, walkers, and skateboarders. Early risers drank coffee at the little café.

As we moved toward the bridge over Storrow, I spotted Vinnie Morris leaning against a large black Mercedes. He was reading a newspaper. A cup of coffee was in his hand.

"Nice suit," Z said.

"It's what a life of crime can buy," I said.

"Something to consider," Z said.

I nodded. I fist-bumped him in our own private joke and walked toward Vinnie. He had on a navy linen suit with a crisp shirt open at the throat and slip-on loafers. As his watch glinted in the sun, I surmised it was probably worth more than my retirement account.

He nodded at me. "You pull a hamstring back there?"

"I was taking it easy on the kid."

"Sure," Vinnie said. "You versus a D-one running back. No contest."

"You bring me a coffee?"

"Of course," Vinnie said. "And there's lobster benedict in the trunk."

"Just passing through?" I said. I turned my torso back and forth and gripped my right foot behind me in a quad stretch. I did the same with the left. Tomorrow I would be sore. But as I'd be relaxing with Susan, it wasn't a major concern.

"What the fuck were you thinking, taking on Davey Stefanakos?"

"It was the first time I'd met Davey," I said. "He seems very nice. Very professional."

"You bet," Vinnie said. "After what you and Hawk did to DeMarco's people last year, he's invested in more quality. Stefanakos will swallow you whole. He was a pro fighter. Beat the hell out of some Russian guy. Nearly killed him and got banned for life."

"Not Ivan Drago," I said. "He brought hope to us all."

"I'd advise you get out of town for a while."

"Already in the works."

"Bullshit."

"Doesn't have anything to do with DeMarco," I said. "It's Susan's birthday. I'm pretty sure DeMarco will still be pissed when I get back."

"You bet he will," Vinnie said. He reached for his coffee, took a sip, and then shook his head. "He may have put some money down on the deal."

"The deal?"

"Your head," Vinnie said. "Your fucking life. You think you're making buddies with DeMarco like you did Tony Marcus and Gino Fish? You guys shake hands and then start sending each other Christmas cards? Christ, not everyone gets soft."

"No one ever accused you of getting soft."

"Damn right," Vinnie said. "It was take over my own crew or get pushed out. I wasn't raised like that. No one pushes me out until I'm ready."

"I agree."

"So watch your back," Vinnie said. "I'll be there if you need me. But I can't be there all the time. Who else knows where you're going?"

"Hawk, Z," I said. "Henry Cimoli."

"And don't tell nobody else," he said. "I'd keep Hawk and Chief Dan George there close. DeMarco thinks you're trying to frame him for that church fire and all these crazy fires."

"I made an inquiry," I said. "Through your pal Tommy Torch."

"Tommy Torch is no friend of mine," he said. "He's a peder-ast lowlife. Looks like he told DeMarco and his crew what you were up to. Must've gone to the highest bidder."

"I didn't offer him anything," I said. "Besides putting in a good word with the D.A. if his info worked out."

"You know how to go right to the criminal's heart."

I nodded. Vinnie offered his hand. As he did so, he looked over his shoulder and then along the Esplanade. Convinced no one was watching, he nodded and got back into the long Mercedes.

I watched him cut up into Beacon Hill as I walked back to my apartment.

Nice to have friends.

D id you kill him?" Kevin said.

"Would you shut the hell up," Johnny said. "Jesus."

"I'm serious," Kevin said. "You need to let me know. Because that makes me part of it. I'm not going to jail for this shit. I just want to help."

"You're already part of it," Johnny said. He lit up a Marlboro Red and blew smoke out the window. They were stuck in traffic on the Neponset Bridge headed over to Quincy. He mashed his horn and pounded the wheel with his fist.

Johnny had to check on a faulty sensor at a packie before they made the rounds tonight and Kevin decided to tag along. Johnny had two places that were perfect in Roxbury and another in Braintree. Johnny had grown up there and knew the streets by heart.

"Just what did Featherstone say to you?"

"Like I said, he saw your vehicle at the warehouse we torched," Kevin said. "I told him it was probably one of your security jobs. But he kept on pushing it."

"Did he mention anything about any cops or guys in Arson?"

"Nope," Kevin said. "I think he kept it to himself. He was just kind of talking out loud."

"He was sure as hell talking to somebody," Johnny said. "I fucking know it. He was asking you about me because he'd already decided what to do. He wanted to play the fucking hero and take me down. He thought you'd be his goat."

"Featherstone wasn't like that," Kevin said. "You could've talked to him. Maybe let him know what we're doing and how it was going to help the whole department. He'd get it."

"Guess we'll never know," Johnnie said. Smiling, smoke leaking out of his nostrils. The traffic moved to a crawl and Johnny reached across him to the glove box. He pulled out a business card and handed it to him.

"Ever heard of this guy?"

"A private eye?" Kevin said. He sort of laughed. "Nope."

"You sure?"

"Are you doubting me?" Kevin said. "I been in this damn thing from the start. So don't get paranoid that everyone is turning. I said I'd stick with it and I'll stick with it. We got the whole department hopping. Things are

gonna get better for them. The city will take care of them. Give them what they need. Where'd you get that card?"

"Found it someplace," Johnny said.

"On Featherstone?"

Johnny mashed his horn and threw up his hands. The car in front of him at a dead stop, traffic moving along ahead into Quincy. The bright summer sun going down over the river.

"We gotta find him," Johnny said. "I know this guy at Engine Eight. He says this guy is a pal of that fat ass Jack McGee. He's seen them together. If this guy knew Featherstone and Featherstone told him about us, we are royally fucked."

"And then where does it stop, Johnny?" Kevin said. "This is to do some good. You can't get nuts on me. This guy doesn't know shit."

"He's not part of the department," Johnny said. "This snoop is a fucking outsider. We need to let him know he's not welcome to any of this."

Johnny moved off the bridge and zipped around the big SUV that had been blocking him for the last ten minutes. He gave an old woman the finger and then reached up with his little hand to puff on the cigarette. He tucked the cigarette back in his mouth as he took a turn.

"And how do we do that?" Kevin said. But already knowing the answer.

"You hit a man where he lives and he'll never get back up."

The next morning, Susan and I lay side by side in lounge chairs facing a large, clover-shaped pool. The pool looked very much the same as it had more than twenty years ago. The hotel not so much. The carpet was dated and the restaurant less than spectacular. Back in the glory days, it was Dunfey's. Now it was just called the Resort and Conference Center at Hyannis.

"Do you think I look that much different?" Susan said.

She wore a strapless black one-piece. Her shoulders and long limbs were toned and tan. Her hair was wet, shiny, and black. Her sunglasses were large and white, looking like something lifted from Audrey Hepburn.

"Not a bit," I said. "But I think I'm taller. And have more stamina."

"You did last night."

"Aren't you impressed I got us the same room?"

"With the same décor," she said. "I guess the hotel is into nostalgia, too."

"Would you rather move to the Chatham Bars?"

"Yes," she said. "But no. We came here for a reason. And it's a very good one."

I had on a pair of black Wayfarers, my Braves cap, and red swim trunks. Sometimes, you don't mess with the classics. "Shall I sing 'Happy Birthday' now or at dinner?"

"Is it just you?" she said. "Or have you arranged for an entire orchestra?"

"The Pops were busy," I said. "How would you feel about Spenser and the Dropkick Murphys? 'Happy Birthday, Dear Suze'?"

Susan lowered her sunglasses a hint, raised an eyebrow, and arched her back before settling into the lounge chair. Outside the pool, a couple of men practiced on a small putting green and talked about what little they knew about athletics. I'd been told there was an excellent golf course on the premises. The problem was that I had never played golf or ever intended to play.

"Enjoy the break," I said. "Things might get complicated when we get home."

"Work?"

I shrugged. I wasn't sure if Susan could even tell, with the big white sunglasses on.

"Anyone particularly mad at you?" she said. "Or too many to count?"

"I may have focused some interest on the wrong man," I said. "Who is a very bad man. Just not the right man for what I suspected."

"You made a mistake?"

"I know," I said. "Can you believe it?"

"And how'd you find out you'd upset him?"

"Vinnie let me know," I said. "He recommended we leave town for a bit."

"Did that annoy you?" she said. "That you had already planned this trip and some might infer it was connected?"

"Very much so."

Susan's attention drifted for a moment. A young woman in a black top and small white shorts walked around the pool, checking on guests. Susan tapped her index finger on her lower lip, deep in thought. "Is it too early for a cocktail?"

I looked at my watch. It was after eleven a.m. I shook my head. "Don't be ridiculous."

Susan ordered a mimosa for her and a Bloody Mary for me. I asked for extra celery and olives to keep it as healthy as possible. As we drank and enjoyed the sun and splashing sounds of the pool, I told her more about the case. I started with Captain Collins and wound my way around to John Grady's confession and on to my recent talk with the arson investigators.

"Cops think whoever is lighting these fires killed Featherstone, the Spark."

"And what do you think?"

"Not sure," I said. "But his wife is sure of it. She says it's the only important thing he's ever done in his life."

"Uncover an arsonist?"

"Get killed by one."

"I once treated a teenager who was obsessed with fire," she said. "He was a true pyromaniac. Through cognitive therapy, I believe I was able to help him."

"What does setting a fire do for a person, doc?"

"This boy had a very high IQ," she said. "But often fire starters aren't very bright. Fire fascinates them. Some are even mentally challenged. Others find an interest in fire during puberty. They find something almost sexual about it."

"Fire and sex seems like a bad match," I said. "The reason I never cook naked."

"Almost never," Susan said.

"Does everything always go back to sex?"

"If you're a shrink?" she said. "You bet it does. I've read in medical journals that the adult who gets consumed by setting fires is driven, much like a sex addict."

"What about us?" I said. "Are we sex addicts?"

"Addiction is only a problem when it causes harm to yourself and those you love."

"Sometimes I believe we traumatize Pearl," I said. "The way she wails and claws at the door. Where will it all lead?"

"Pearl is a mature girl."

"True."

"Does Jack McGee believe the church fire was set to harm firefighters?"

"Yes."

"And have there been other church fires?"

"Two," I said. "But one was proven electrical. Most have been warehouses."

"Were they both Catholic churches?"

"The electrical was at a Presbyterian church."

"I guess you have to separate the arsonist who sets fire for so-called legitimate reasons," she said. "Revenge, extortion. Sometimes a teenager is just seeking thrills. I would venture to guess a true pyromaniac is a small fraction of those who engage in this type behavior."

"There is some nut sending notes to arson investigators calling himself Mr. Firebug," I said. "They've got dozens of notes. They always send them to the ATF lab, but whoever sent the note, whether authentic or not, seems to know what they're doing. No fingerprints. Very common household printer."

"Mr. Firebug?"

"Catchy."

"If he's real, he likes power."

"Of course."

"And notoriety."

"Sure."

"Is he good at his job?"

"Setting fires?"

"Yes."

"Captain Cahill certainly thinks so," I said.

Susan drank some of her mimosa. I shook the ice in the Bloody Mary to squeeze out a few last sips. I popped an olive into my mouth and crossed my legs at the ankles. The golfers had moved on and we were left with the sound of the wind. A few gulls glided over the golf course.

"Has Jack considered the firebug may be one of his own?"

"I have," I said. "But to Jack, that would be akin to blasphemy."

"What happened to your Bloody Mary?" she said.

"I needed to replenish my vitamins and minerals," I said. "You're not easy, kid. I plan on getting a dozen oysters for lunch."

Susan lay back, stretched her legs, and gave a soft sigh. She did not speak for a long while as the sun warmed our bodies. I drank another Bloody Mary. A short time later, Susan strolled back to our room, crooking a finger in my direction.

awoke to a ringing phone and a perky woman at the front desk telling me I had a visitor. Before I could ask who, she hung up. Susan was already in the shower getting ready for dinner.

I slipped on a pair of khakis and a navy blue T-shirt, sliding on a .38 in a holster behind my hip. The T-shirt was long and loose and draped over the outline of the gun. I sauntered down the hallway and into the wide lobby. The lobby was bright and utilitarian, with blue chairs and sofas and a busy carpet that might have impressed Jackson Pollock.

I spotted two women in tennis outfits chatting and the man I'd seen earlier from the putting green. He was busy with two young boys who raced around the lobby. No one was at the front desk, so I ducked into the bar to take a peek.

Hawk leaned against the bar like Alan Ladd in *Shane*. Instead of buckskin, he had on a blue floral jacket, white jeans, and blue oxford shoes. The floral pattern had been woven in navy upon white material. Underneath, he wore a crisp white linen shirt.

"Does Miss Scarlett know you made a mess out of her drapes?"

"Ha," Hawk said. "This here is a Billy Reid. What you call couture."

"Sharper than when I saw you here last."

"King Powers." Hawk grinned. He looked to be sipping a gin and tonic. "Folks lookin' for you in Boston."

"I know."

"Had to reason with a couple at the gym."

"How'd you do?"

"As always."

"You see Stefanakos?"

"That big-ass Greek?"

I nodded.

"No," he said. "Been waiting on it. You and him got some unfinished business."

I nodded and took a seat on the bar stool. Hawk sipped his drink. "You don't think they'll come here?"

Hawk shrugged. "Depends on who you told."

"You, Z, and Henry."

Hawk nodded. "I guess I made a long drive for nothing."

"You could've just called."

"No answer," Hawk said.

"Hmm." I smiled and scratched my head. "Maybe I turned it off."

"Just try not to break or pull anything."

I asked the bartender for a Harpoon IPA on draft. Next to Hawk, I looked slovenly and wrinkled. I had on Top-Siders and I needed a shave. I looked like I might belong on *Gilligan's Island*. He didn't seem to mind and ordered another gin and tonic. Extra limes.

"Don't want to get in the way of your, uh, retreat."

"Join us for dinner," I said. "It's Susan's birthday. Although I'm not sure she's thrilled with the prospect."

"Susan look too good to worry about a number," he said.

"I think we're both aware that Z could quite respectably be our son," I said.

"No way a thick-necked honkie and a Jewish shrink can make a full-blooded Cree Indian."

"You make an excellent point."

Hawk drank some more from the glass. I drank my beer and ordered another. By the time the bartender set down the glass, Susan walked into the room. She'd showered and changed into a black maxi-dress. Her hair was in a tight bun, accentuating the diamond studs in her ears. My heart felt like Gene Krupa was practicing in my chest.

"Mm-mm," Hawk said.

She kissed him on the cheek and took a seat between us.

"Hawk was in the neighborhood."

"I know what it means," she said. "Anyone else coming?"

Hawk grinned. "Ain't nobody here but us chickens."

Susan joined Hawk with a vodka gimlet. He began to softly whistle "Happy Birthday." She slugged him in the arm.

I showered, shaved, and changed into a pair of crisp jeans and a short-sleeved black polo. Thirty minutes later, we were having dinner at a place called the Naked Oyster on Main Street. The building was long and narrow, with bright, splashy paintings hung on brick walls. An oyster bar ran against the wall with shellfish in ice waiting to be shucked.

We ate outside, directly across from the JFK museum and post office. The night was warm, but a nice breeze came off the water. The air smelled like the sea. Families strolled by eating ice cream and eyeing all the boutiques lit up on Main. Susan ordered tuna tartare, Hawk had the duck confit, and I decided on a plate of haddock tacos.

"What if Hawk had snuck up on you?" Susan said. "Someone could've been hurt."

"Impossible," I said. "I have a sixth sense. Besides, how's he going to sneak up in that jacket?"

"I like it," Susan said. "It looks terrific on you."

Hawk grinned. He nodded in appreciation of Susan's style.

"Can you stay?" she said.

"Nope," Hawk said. "Just came down to warn white boy about some trouble in River City."

"Helps you cultivate horse sense and a cool head and a keen eye," I said. "Bad?"

Hawk shook his head. "Just wind."

"About the arson?" Susan said.

Hawk shook his head. "More about Jackie DeMarco's pride," Hawk said. "Man can't have anyone questioning what he does."

"Has he ever met you two?" Susan said. "You question everyone's pride."

Hawk looked to me and smiled. "She got a point."

An appetizer of oysters arrived, French-style, on a bed of salt with a mignonette. Hawk and I split the order. Susan had a rare second gimlet. "Cut it with Rose's lime," I said. "Half and with half gin. Terry Lennox says it beats martinis hollow."

Susan and Hawk ignored me. Hawk drained the oyster off each shell without spilling a drop on his jacket. Susan drained maybe two teaspoons of the gimlet. Hawk checked out a young woman in a long black skirt and a revealing white tank top.

Hawk could check out a woman so furtively she never knew. Unless he wanted her to know.

We ate and laughed. We talked about old times in Cambridge, Montecito, and Vegas. Not one word was mentioned about our time in Mill River. The food came. We ate and drank. I tipped the waitress to add a bunch of sparklers atop a large slice of key lime pie.

Susan distributed three forks for the piece. She pointed hers directly at my chest. "Anyone tries to sing and they'll get hurt," she said.

Hawk and I did not disagree.

Two days later, I was up late watching a movie in which Gary Cooper plays Marco Polo; Susan and Pearl were fast asleep in bed. Just as Marco Polo had discovered gunpowder and spaghetti, Frank Belson called.

"Where are you?" he said.

"Susan's."

"You got some trouble at your apartment."

"I do have a restraining order against Kate Upton."

"No joke," he said. "Your buddy McGee and half of Boston Fire are fighting a five-alarm on Marlborough. I'm here. It ain't pretty."

Fifteen minutes later, I parked illegally on Arlington by the Public Garden. Several blocks of Marlborough had been closed off by police. Flames shot up high from the row house where I'd lived for years. I walked to the barricade at the corner of Arlington and Marlborough and spotted Jack McGee.

He sat on the back of an ambulance, taking in oxygen. He had soot across his face and hands.

"Everybody out?" I said.

He nodded, still pressing the oxygen mask against his face.

"You sure?"

He took off the mask. "Be my guest to double check."

McGee told the cops to let me inside the barricade. He had on the heavy black coat and pants with a helmet affixed on his large head. "Call came in about an hour ago," he said. "We got six companies on this. If we can cool down the walls, we can stop it spreading. Already went into both buildings beside yours. We got it contained."

"How's mine?"

"Sorry." McGee shook his head. "It's gone, Spenser."

We walked together toward my building, the street clogged with at least six different engines. Firefighters sprayed through broken windows, arcing water up toward the third floor and roof. My window turret remained, but there was no glass. I could only see blackness inside. The street ran slick with water, flashing lights reflecting in puddles. I swallowed, my insides feeling hollow.

"Maybe I can salvage some underwear and that Duke Snider rookie card."

"Anything irreplaceable?" McGee said.

"Everything's replaceable," I said.

"No one's dead," McGee said. "But two of our guys got sent to Mass General."

My mouth felt dry. I felt selfish for thinking about my record collection, baseball cards, clothes, photographs, oil paintings, and good china. A Schott jacket Susan had bought me. A wood-working tool given to me by my late uncle Cash. A well-loved Winchester 20-20 that belonged to my father and his grandfather before him.

"I'm sorry, Spenser," McGee said.

I nodded. "Awfully bold."

"DeMarco?"

I shook my head. "He'd come straight for me," I said. "Not like this. He'd just shoot me in the back."

"If it's DeMarco, I'll kill him myself," McGee said. "This is some kind of fucked-up game."

On the sidewalk across from my apartment, I saw a youngish woman hoisting a little girl in pajamas in her arms. A man stood close to them talking feverishly on a cell phone. He was crying and yelling at the same time. An elderly woman in a tired red robe who lived on the first floor of my building sat on the curb. Her face was blank as she stared up openmouthed at the flames, her gray hair frizzy and wild as she clutched a shoebox.

"Fucking bastards," McGee said.

"Yep," I said.

I could feel the heat like a sunburn on my face, smell the scent of burning hair. I stepped back as more firefighters stepped forward to dampen the whole mess. My apartment appeared to be completely gone. The two buildings that sandwiched it appeared to have been saved. McGee rejoined his men.

Another fire truck drove down the street slow with lights and sirens. Two men jumped from the truck, extended a flat yellow hose, and ran toward a hydrant. Several firefighters scaled a ladder to the roof of my building with oxygen tanks on their back. I saw Capelletti from Arson get close up the steps to my building and fire off some shots with his camera.

A little while later, Teddy Cahill arrived in street clothes and a ball cap. The men walked inside.

I walked in the opposite direction, past the EMTs, firefighters, and cops to Arlington. My body and brain felt numb. But I was alive. Susan was alive.

"You okay?" said a female cop by her patrol car.

"Yeah." I stopped and nodded. "Still here."

35

With no sleep, some breakfast, and a little coffee, things looked much worse in the daylight.

I stood in the middle of Marlborough Street with Teddy Cahill. I'd brought Pearl with me, and she sat on her haunches as we peered up at the charred mess. Pearl sniffed at the smoky remnants in the air while the apartment building continued to smolder. I was fortunate to always keep several changes of clothes at Susan's. Sometimes fresh underwear is better than a cup of coffee.

"What do we have?" I said.

"Been working all night," Cahill said. "ATF sent some good people over. We went over your place inch by fucking inch."

"And?"

"At least we know where this one started," Cahill said. "Two places. One right by your fucking door and the other on a back wall in the alley. We got a few witnesses who saw a white van parked out back for a few minutes. But no one saw who went inside."

"Can I see my place?"

"We got a lot of guys working."

"I'll step lightly," I said. "As will Pearl."

We walked to Arlington and then back down the Public Alley 421. The back side of the apartment building was damaged worse than the front. Firefighters continued to dampen the roofs and top floors of my building. Smoke broke and scattered in the wind.

Cahill got onto his haunches and showed the alligator-like marks along some siding, stretching several feet higher and toward the basement door.

"Looks like they used some tires to get it going hot," he said. "You can see the remnants on the asphalt."

"A white van?"

"Woman in the apartment directly behind you saw it blocking the alley," Cahill said. He rubbed his walrus mustache. "But didn't see anyone come or go."

Pearl looked up at me and tilted her head. She was on high alert for clues, her eyes full of worry and confusion.

"We found a few things," he said. "ATF will run some tests."

"And what are the chances it matches with Mr. Firebug?"

"Who needs to run a test?" he said. "But why'd they pick on you?"

"I don't think it was a secret I talked to Featherstone before he died," I said. "They may have conflated me, Arson unit, and Homicide. One-stop shopping."

I ran my hands along the charred siding and looked up at the back of my building. I patted Pearl's head. Her nubbed tail wagged.

"Got somewhere to stay?" Cahill said.

"Yeah," I said. "With a friend."

"Your friend okay with the dog?" he said. "If not, I can take her for a while. Galway likes other hounds."

"I think my friend likes the dog better than me," I said. "Is it possible to walk upstairs?"

"Sure," he said. "But you don't want to see it. I promise there's nothing left."

"It's important."

Cahill nodded. We walked into the gaping mouth of the back door to the landing and up a back stairwell dripping with water. Pearl sniffed at the charred carpet and piles of charred wood. The sprinklers had done a lot of damage to the halls and the stairwell. Cahill told me he wouldn't take responsibility if we fell right through the floor. He took me to my floor and swept his hand toward what had been my apartment. It was hard to tell. There was no door. A large portion of the wall facing Marlborough had dissolved. I stepped through the soggy, blackened mess. A firefighter on a ladder waved to me as he made his way up to a higher floor.

Pearl knew she was home. She turned her mournful yellow eyes on me.

My bookshelf wasn't just burned. It simply was no longer there. I found a couple half-eaten picture frames and some cast-iron cookware. Tough stuff, forged in flame. Cahill advised me to leave it until the insurance people could take pictures.

"They could have my ass for letting you in."

I walked back to the bedroom and turned straight around. I stepped carefully around the hole in the kitchen and returned to the fireplace. On the hearth, I found a toppled piece of wood I'd once carved into a horse. It still looked a little like a horse but was much smaller and much blacker. I slipped it into my pocket. Pearl began to whimper. I walked to where the shelving had been to hold the old Winchester. I found the gun a real mess, but the barrel and level held their shape.

"Just what will you need to link all these fires?"

"We have a working theory," he said. "But it's very technical."

"It didn't sound technical to me the other night," I said. "You seemed pretty damn sure it was the work of the same person or persons."

"Sometimes I envy Homicide," he said. "They have real evidence. We work with nothing but fucking chemicals and ashes. Unless we get someone to turn, we don't have much. I'm sorry about your place. But while we were hosing down the Back Bay, someone else touched off another place in the South End. By the time we got a company over there, six of our people were at Mass General for burns and smoke inhalation. We're pretty sure your place was a diversion."

"How bad are they hurt?"

"They will be back soon," he said. "But one guy may be looking at retirement."

I nodded and swallowed. My apartment and possessions no longer mattered. "Again," I said. "How do you know it's the same guy?"

"He's got a way of doing things," he said. "Let's leave it at that."

"You think I'm going to publish a piece in *The Globe*?"

"If word gets out, he might change things," he said. "Right now he's got a system. We upset the system and we upset our case."

"What's the system?"

"Found stuff here that looks just like Holy Innocents," he said. "Okay? Between us, we think he makes a device from a paper grocery bag and plastic Baggie full of kerosene. We found a butt of match at both places and traces of the Baggie. ATF can tell us what kind of accelerant was used."

"Any new letters?"

"Nope," he said. "But we will. Or the TV station will. That's where he sends them."

"Which station?"

Cahill told me and we walked out of my apartment and carefully down the steps and back out to the alley. A warm wind blew through the narrow space as we made our way toward the Public Garden. Several news crews had set up for the day along the wrought-iron fencing.

All the cameras pointed directly at my former home.

I met Hank Phillippi Ryan an hour later at Government Center. Hank worked as an investigative reporter for WHBH, the NBC affiliate that had studios nearby on Bulfinch Place. She took a seat with me on a concrete bench with a nice view of the soulless brick piazza. I brought her a coffee the way she liked it. Skim milk with one sugar.

I gave her my best smile, the one that showed my white teeth and dimples. "Help me, Hank."

She reached out and hugged me. I was careful not to spill the coffee. "I'm so sorry."

"I can stay with Susan for a while," I said. "She promises reasonable rent and fringe benefits."

Hank was a tall woman with ash-blond hair and dark eyes. She had on a black wrap dress and a simple string of pearls. "And then what?"

"I'll hunt for a new place," I said. "Living together isn't an option for us."

I handed Hank the coffee. She thanked me and we watched a huge gathering not far from the T station. There had been several shootings over the weekend in Roxbury. Many walked to the central plaza with signs reading BLACK LIVES MATTER. The coffee and the commotion in the plaza thankfully distracted her.

"I interviewed the family of one of the kids," she said. "He was only fourteen and ambushed by two older kids. He'd been sent to the corner store by his mother."

"Never stops."

"Nope," she said. "But I wish to God it would. We've seen a few things in this city. I guess you wanted to ask me about another neighborhood. Your Mr. Firebug?"

"Yep."

"I guess I should be flattered," Hank said. "All the psychopaths adore me."

"Lucky you."

"How'd you know about the letters?" she said. "We decided not to report on them. It's obviously what he wants. It's our station policy not to give that kind of publicity. We turned them over to Boston Fire."

"Teddy Cahill told me," I said. "He says they're authentic."

"I know," Hank said. "But did Teddy tell you that he's given details of the fire that only the arsonists would know?"

"That he did not."

"This guy may be a loon, but he's careful," Hank said. "No prints. Nothing they can use yet."

"Do we have to be gender-specific?" I said. "Maybe Mr. Firebug is a ruse. Maybe it's Miss Firebug."

"Sounds like an exotic dancer," she said. "How about the insurance angle?"

"I tried to follow the money trail," I said. "But that didn't pan out. In the process, I may have angered some local wise guys."

"If you don't piss off a few people each day, what's the use of getting up?"

I toasted her with my coffee. I leaned forward on the bench. More protesters walked across the plaza to join the rally. A man with a bullhorn began to speak. We listened to what he had to say and it made a great deal of sense. The movement began to march toward city hall. We waited as it passed until we spoke again.

"You know this guy has done dozens of fires," Hank said. "And he promises much more until he gets what he wants."

"What does he want?"

"The funny thing about crazies is that he hasn't really said."

"Did you keep copies of the letters?"

Hank returned the question with a look that seemed to appraise my intelligence.

"May I see the copies?"

"Of course."

We sat in the hot, shadeless expanse of Government Center. I'd sweated through my T-shirt as if I'd run a marathon. I did not detect a note of perspiration on Hank. It must be a TV reporter's trick of the trade.

"I have another favor," I said.

"Of course you do."

"Do you think I only come to you when I need something?"

"You know, I was having lunch with Rita Fiore just the other day at Trade," Hank said. "And we were discussing this very thing."

"I have done plenty of things for Rita," I said.

"You know, she was saying exactly the opposite."

"I can imagine the way Rita would say it."

"What's the favor?" Hank said. She absently looked at her phone and then at the thin watch on her wrist.

"I want to look at video of the fires."

"Which fires?"

"Every fire that is suspect."

"That's a lot," she said. "This guy has been burning Boston since the first of the year."

"And maybe beyond that," I said.

Hank raised her eyebrows. I lifted up a hand. "The more I know, the more I can share."

"You better."

I crossed my heart and held up my right hand. "I think this all started last year," I said. "I think Mr. Firebug got started with the old church but got scared and stopped. Now he's revved back up for the summer season."

"Arson already went through our video," she said. "I figured if they'd found something, they'd have asked for copies. They were here for a few hours and then didn't come back."

"Maybe I'll see something they didn't," I said. "I do have a keen, appraising eye."

"Knock yourself out," she said. "I can get you a private room to watch the raw footage."

"You mind if I sleep there, too?"

"I'm sure Susan won't place a time limit on you," she said. "But if she does, I know Rita would make room in her bed."

"You know, she's only bluffing."

"You really believe that?" Hank raised her eyebrows again. We stood and shook hands, and she walked off without saying good-bye.

Although he wouldn't remain under my tutelage for long, I knew watching endless hours of video was the perfect training exercise for Z. At first, he seemed skeptical. But I enticed him with the promise of grinders from Quincy Market and free coffee from the TV station canteen.

"Yippee," he said.

"A dream come true."

"You think it'll be more glamorous in Los Angeles?"

"City of Angels," I said. "What do you think? It's probably a law you get a massage on a stakeout. Herbal tea during a car chase."

"I've heard the rumors," he said. "They must be true."

"How many hours have we logged?" I said. The room was dark and cold. It seemed as if we'd been there since the early 1970s. I had not seen Hank, but one of her producers had checked on us twice. One brought coffee. Another donuts. God bless them.

"Eighteen fires," he said. "We've been here for six hours."

"Keep track of time for your invoices."

"Are you invoicing Jack McGee?" Z said.

I shrugged, took a sip of coffee, and asked him to continue on with the video. Even though it wasn't tape anymore, it was a digital image housed on a TV station server. I was a long way from watching Super 8 with my football coach and the whir and click of the machine. Z worked a mouse to stop, freeze, and zoom in. After a while, everything looked the same. Not every fire had been filmed by WHDH, only the nastiest ones. Most of the footage showed the firefighters doing their thing and then a standup from the public-information guy, Steve MacDonald. Sometimes Commissioner Foley would take questions from reporters. We fast-forwarded through all the talk. We were looking at the onlookers. I hoped that somewhere the arsonist would show his face and return to do so again. If we could spot a face in the crowd more than once, we might just have a pattern.

"That guy," Z said. "I saw him from an earlier fire. Tall, goofy guy. Kind of balding."

He backed up the video. It was Rob Featherstone.

"He's dead," I said. "But let's see who he's with."

Z ran it for several seconds and then froze the frame. I asked Z to make a screen grab of the image. It was Featherstone and two other men handing out bottles of water. Featherstone and other men who must have been Sparks appeared at several of the fires. At first glance, they would have been dismissed by anyone familiar with fire scenes. But now, with Featherstone dead, it was worth taking another look at the company he kept.

"So they are like fans," Z said, "only for firemen?"

"Yep."

"And they go to fires and try to assist."

"Yep."

"When I played football, we had many women who wanted to assist us."

"I bet."

"My girlfriend wanted to assist me morning and night until I got benched," he said. "And then she wanted to assist someone else."

"That's why sometimes one must assist oneself."

"Are you always filled with such wisdom?"

"How will you make it without me?"

The video moved ahead, showing a warehouse in flames and firefighters shooting water into the guts of the building. Z clicked on another thumbnail image for an apartment fire from March. He let the unedited video run. He skipped through the standup and moved on from the tight footage of the burning building, firefighters, and EMTs. Nothing new. We skipped a couple fires, as they did not match those suspected by Cahill. I wanted to see only fires considered for arson. Several fires, including one where six people died, were accidental. If we didn't get what we needed, we could go back and look at those, too.

I got up and stretched. Z and I walked over to Quincy Market for some coffee and grinders. The donut talk had really gotten our appetites going. We watched another three hours of footage, walked to the Harbor Health Club, and worked out on the heavy bag and with mitts.

I drove back home and had dinner with Susan.

The next morning, we were at it again.

An hour into the last several months, Z stopped a quick pan to a crowd. The shot was only two or three seconds. But with the digital video, we could zoom in tight. Z stood up and stretched and pointed at the large computer monitor. "You see that?"

"See what?"

"The man pointed a gun in the air."

I looked closer and saw just the glint of a metallic object flash and then disappear. Z pressed slow forward and it became clear it was a gun. A man brandished a pistol for a second, a large smile crossing his face. It appeared the two men with him were laughing and smiling.

"They're celebrating," I said.

"Yep," Z said. "Eight families out of an apartment in Southie. They may not be arsonists, but they are guilty of being ass-holes."

"Why would anyone celebrate a fire?"

Z captured several still images. He zoomed in very close to the men's faces.

The late Rob Featherstone's second-in-command, Jerry Ramaglia, met me across from the Boston Fire Museum at
Flour Bakery. I bought us two coffees and found a somewhat secluded table by a picture window fronting Farnsworth.
It was late. The light had turned a soft summer gold on the old
warehouses and garages.

"I heard what happened to your place," Ramaglia said. "I'm
sorry. If we can do anything. Or help any of the tenants."

I thanked him. Between us sat a lemon meringue pie to share
with Susan tonight in lieu of rent. She, too, recognized Joanne
Chang's particular genius. My Braves cap rested on the box to
stake my claim.

"Someone believes Rob left his suspicions with me," I said.

"I know," he said. "Rob's wife is screwy, but I think she's right
about this. He got shot in the back and dumped off a bridge.

What's the matter with this city? The man only wanted to help others. He was a freakin' saint."

I resisted the urge to open the box and start in on the pie with both hands. Restraint.

"How long have you been a Spark?" I said.

"Twenty-two years," he said. "Loved every minute."

I slid the stills from a large manila mailer and set them on the table between us. "Recognize these men?"

Ramaglia reached into his shirt pocket and pulled out a pair of cheaters. Had I not been in public, I might have reached for mine. He studied the first photo for a while and then flipped through the rest. He shuffled them in a neat pile and placed them on the envelope. "Jesus Christ."

"Know them?"

"Yes, sir," he said. "Afraid I do."

"Are they Sparks?"

"Hell, no," he said. "Thank God. The young guy's name is Teehan. I don't know his first name. He runs with this guy Johnny Donovan who's a bad seed. He tried to join the association for at least ten years. About three years ago, he came to our meeting unannounced and basically told Rob that he was a fucking asshole. I hadn't seen him much since, but I know he's still out there, trying to say he's a Spark. He drives a big red Chevy SUV, pretending he's official or something. A first-class Froot Loop. Someone should bring him up on charges."

"Is he violent?"

"I don't think so," Ramaglia said. "Just a nut. Why? You think these are the guys?"

"They were observed acting very strange at a few fire scenes."

"They are strange," Ramaglia said. "But I don't see them shooting Rob in the back. Teehan is a blowhard. But he loves firefighters. He wouldn't torch a building and put the boys in danger. The guy who killed Rob lit those fires and burned you out, too."

"You know where I can find them?"

"Donovan runs some kind of security business in Southie," Ramaglia said. "I know he's a rent-a-cop of some sort. Always has a badge and a gun."

"What about Teehan?"

"He's just a kid," Ramaglia said. "Jesus, I don't know. Probably still lives with his mother. I can ask around."

"Is he friendly with any of the Sparks?"

"A few," Ramaglia said. "You know, he's a good kid if he kept different company."

"Can you ask around without mentioning me or that anyone is asking about him?"

"Sure."

I drank some coffee. I continued to resist the urge to eat part of the pie. I even had silverware within reach. If I worked out a sliver, Susan wouldn't even notice. It had been a hard week. I deserved some pie.

"What about the third man?" I said. "Do you know him?"

Ramaglia shook his head. "I may have seen him hanging around," he said. "Can I keep one of those pictures?"

"Absolutely," I said. "But keep this circle tight."

Ramaglia drank some coffee. It felt very good to be in the air-conditioning and drinking hot beverages. I planned to stop back by the new farmers' market again tonight. That place was the best thing to hit Boston since Carl Yastrzemski. I also could use several new shirts, khakis, and jeans. Underwear, socks, bullets.

"Rob's wife's not doing so good," Ramaglia said. He looked out the window at a group of children from a summer day camp jumping and jostling. "She held up good for the wake and all. But now it's over, she's a fucking mess. They were together a long time."

The kids continued to make a lot of noise, like a crazy parade, and continued toward the waiting doors of a school bus. Everyone waited in a neat and orderly line for the bus to let them inside. A few of them pounded on the side of the bus; others took in the scenery around them.

"Call me if you can find out about the third guy," I said. "Or get a first name on Teehan that I could check out."

"Rob was good people. Ain't nobody deserves to die like that. Whoever did this and torched your apartment is a real coward. I sure hope you can help."

"Yeah," I said. "Me, too."

39

Pearl barked and circled as I entered with bags from Whole Foods and set them on the upstairs kitchen counter. Susan had on a loose linen skirt and a navy silk tank, her hair piled in a messy bun on top of her head.

"How bad is the apartment?" she said. She stood in front of me, placing both hands on my face. She wanted to look into my eyes.

"Do you remember that fantastic white suit I used to wear?"

"Do I?"

"Whoosh," I said. "Gone."

"Oh, thank God," she said. "And the black leather trench coat?"

"All the old wardrobe is gone."

"Hmm," she said. "Maybe there is an upside."

"If I don't go shopping or do some laundry, I may have to dip into your closet."

"There's a little give in some of my wrap dresses," she said. "But not that much."

"How about I cook dinner and we can discuss?"

"A roomie with benefits?"

I rolled my chambray shirt up to my elbows and started to wash the greens. They were local and very fresh. I let them drain in a colander and laid out the rest of the salad: a carrot, a purple onion, red pepper, and some candied walnuts. I mixed some Creole mustard with some olive oil and balsamic vinegar as requested by Susan and placed the baguette in the oven to warm.

As it heated, I opened a beer and began to stir up some pimento cheese. I grated a nice hunk of smoked cheddar from American Provisions, added a bit of cream cheese, some Blue Plate mayo, and pimentos. I liked to use a lot of black pepper and some spices from Boudreaux's.

"Don't worry," I said. "I'll stop by Ball and Buck tomorrow for some shirts. I'll need some new workout gear, too."

"And pants, socks, shoes, new furniture, and a place to live."

"Oh," I said. "And that, too."

I made the salad and set the table. I sliced the bread for sandwiches from the hot baguette. She turned off the television and joined me in the dining room. I continued on my Narragansett kick while eating two large sandwiches and a side salad. I had yet to tell her about the lemon meringue.

"Have you learned anything new?"

"After two days of watching video at the TV station, we turned up a couple of suspects."

"That's promising."

The sandwiches were so good, I immediately began to make

more. I set two small ones out for Susan while I let Pearl lick the bowl.

"Both of them have ties to the fire department," I said. "One of them is just a kid. He wants to be a Boston firefighter."

"Starting off as an arsonist won't look good on his application."

"If it's who I believe, I can't figure out what they hope to accomplish," I said. "I'm going to talk to the younger one tomorrow. He seems the most promising."

"And the other?"

"Not so much," I said. "Other than the fact that he is a frustrated wannabe firefighter and the Sparks Association people thought he was a total nutjob. And he once screamed at a man who's now been murdered."

"Haven't we all?"

"There's a third man who was seen with them. But no one knows who he is."

"Harry Lime?"

I lifted an eyebrow and drank some beer. Pearl had finished with the bowl but continued to nose it around the kitchen floor. I picked it up and set it in the sink to wash.

"We believe there's three of them," I said. "If I can get just one to talk, it'll all come apart."

"If one out of three isn't a complete sociopath," she said. "After all they've done."

I nodded. "I can't imagine they wanted it to go this far," I said. "Three firefighters dead."

"And a man who supported the department."

"Any recommendations on talking with the kid?"

Susan poured some Riesling from the refrigerator. She leaned against the counter. "It's pretty much the same as you did with Z," she said. "Find the person he looks up to and destroy the image."

"This creep is no Jumbo Nelson," I said. "And Z had a heart. And brains."

"The power of three," she said. "There's always one who might feel ostracized. The trick is finding out who."

"And why."

found Kevin Teehan working in the garden section of a Home Depot in Somerville. I'd spent the morning learning as much as I could about him. He was twenty-two, a high school dropout, had earned two misdemeanor charges for assault, and he was a longtime volunteer with the fire department in Blackburn. I recognized him from a Facebook photo I'd found online. He posted a lot of photos about firefighting and his mother, who I gathered had died when he was young.

Teehan was a little guy, short and skinny, with a wisp of a beard like Shaggy on *Scooby-Doo*. The closer I got, I saw he'd buzz-cut his dark hair and had quite a collection of acne scars on his face. He wore small studs in each earlobe. Hip.

He watered several flats of white and pink impatiens. The impatiens were now on summer sale.

Teehan stopped watering as I walked close, smiled, and asked if he might help me. I introduced myself and the smile lessened a bit. "I understand you help out Boston Fire sometimes," I said. "I'm hoping you might be able to help me."

"Who are you?" he said.

"I'm working on the fire at the Holy Innocents last year."

"Yeah?" he said. "Don't know how I can help. I work in Blackburn." He looked at me for a long moment and then continued his watering duties. He'd moved on from the impatiens to buckets of lantana. If I hadn't been a gumshoe, perhaps I could've been a botanist.

"But you're sometimes at fire scenes in the city?" I said. "Working with the Sparks?"

He shook his head. "I'm not with the Sparks."

"Why not?"

He craned his head, openmouthed, and shrugged. "Sometimes I've been to some fires around Boston. I like to watch those guys work. You know, to learn stuff."

Teehan's eyes were set too close together. The wispy beard on his chin looked ridiculous. I wanted to grab some pruning shears and do the kid a favor. "What do you learn, Kevin?" I said. Mr. Friendly.

"You see how they work as a team," he said. "It's like a ball game. All fires have a strategy. These guys are top athletes, really."

"What about setting fires?" I said. "Have you learned much about arson?"

He didn't turn to me this time, just kept on running the water over the flowers, nice and easy. "What do you mean?"

"You might have seen something or someone at one of the fires this summer," I said. "You weren't fighting the fire, but you were an educated spectator. You might have noticed a very important detail."

Teehan set down the hose; the nozzle shut off, but water continued to leak on the concrete. The department smelled strongly of soil and fertilizer and the soft sweetness of roses. He brushed some dirt off his orange vest as he studied my face and looked as if he'd decided I was all right. I wondered if he might ever drive a white van.

"How'd you get my name?"

"I interviewed several members of the Sparks," I said. "Rob Featherstone."

Teehan nodded along, playing a bit with the wisps on his chin. "He's dead," Teehan said. "Got fucking carjacked or something. It was on the news. They had a big thing for him at the museum."

"Did you go?" I said.

"No," he said. "I had to work. But he was a good guy. One of the Sparks who actually took time to talk to me."

"I bet you've seen some big fires."

"I've been watching fires since I was a kid," Teehan said. He smiled big. "I always wanted to be a fireman. My mom used to take me to fires when I was a kid. All she could talk about was that someday I'd be on the job."

"You were close?"

"Yeah," he said. "Still are. I bring her flowers every week. Keep her grave fresh like she'd want."

"So why'd you join the department all the way in Blackburn?" I said.

"I took a test for Boston," he said. "I did real good. I'm on the list. But I don't have no family in the department. And I'm not a freakin' woman or black."

I nodded as if I could really identify with his plight of being a young white man in America. "So did you happen to be at the Holy Innocents?"

Teehan actually placed two fingers on his lips, seeming to think on that name. He slowly shook his head. "Nah," he said. "I don't think so."

"You know, the big one?" I said. "Three Boston firefighters died? Dougherty, Bonnelli, and Mulligan? They got trapped in the church basement."

"Yeah, I know. But I wasn't there. I didn't see it."

Although I hadn't seen him on that video, it would be easy enough to check. That morning, I'd culled some of the screen grabs from the footage. I had Z crop some of the faces from different fire scenes, most notably Johnny Donovan. I pulled out a 4x6 with a decent shot of Donovan's face and showed it to Teehan.

"Know this guy?"

Teehan craned his head to study the picture a bit. He did a little more method acting, biting his lip before shaking his head. "Nope."

"You've never seen him?"

Teehan shook his head. "No," he said. "Why?"

"Oh," I said. "Just another onlooker. I think he had a pretty good vantage point at the fire. I hoped he might be able to help me, too. If his name comes to you, just let me know."

"What are you looking for?" he said. "You hearing something?"

I took a deep breath. A curly-headed woman in a pink shirt headed down the aisle pushing a shopping cart. She rested her beefy arms on the cart handle, moving slowly and checking out her seasonal options. She stopped and picked up a pot of blue hydrangeas.

"What about the fire the other night on Marlborough Street?" I said.

He stopped pulling on the thin beard and scratched the back of his neck. "You mean by the Public Garden?"

"Yeah," I said. "Right by the garden. Two firefighters got hurt. Whoever is setting this stuff is getting really reckless. You know?"

I stared at him and I saw fear in his narrow eyes. But he just shook his head and looked away from me, unable to keep contact. "I can ask around," Teehan said. "You got a card or something?"

"You know, Kevin," I said. "For you, I just might."

I pulled one from my wallet and handed it to him. This time I wished I really had the one with the skull-and-crossbones logo.

Yes, I know Johnny Donovan," said a guy named Mark Schultze. "Wish to God I could say I didn't. My experience with him wasn't pleasant."

We sat in his office at a very tony private school in Watertown called Oak Grove. Outside his window, children were conducting some type of summer science camp in a marsh. A table had been set along a boardwalk with microscopes. I imagined summer camp at Oak Grove cost as much as yachting at Martha's Vineyard.

"How long did you know him?" I said.

"He was here when I took the job four years ago," Schultze said. He was a smallish guy with brown hair and an expanding belly. He wore a red gingham shirt that looked like a tablecloth at an Italian restaurant and blocky black eyeglasses. "His official title was security, but he turned out to be more of a fix-it guy. He took care of the heating and cooling, basic maintenance of the property."

"Tell me about the problems you had with him," I said.

"Should I speak to my lawyer before I do?"

"Do you wish to look out for Donovan's interests?"

"Of course not."

I smiled big. "Well, then."

"Six months after I got here," he said. "A few computers disappeared, an iPad or two, and then a large-screen television."

"Did you confront him?"

"Oh, yes," Schultze said. "He was incredulous. Donovan claimed he was part of some witch hunt and blamed some of our landscapers who did not speak English nor had access to the classrooms. He kept on saying it was those rotten Mexicans."

"Did you fire him?"

"Not at first," Schultze said. "He threatened us with a lawsuit if he was reprimanded. That's how the whole adventure started. I should have followed my instincts. I should gotten rid of him immediately."

I raised my eyebrows. I sometimes did this in place of saying "Please continue."

"Are you in contact with anyone in the media, Mr. Spenser?" Schultze said.

"If you're concerned about school privacy, this conversation is between us," I said. "I'm doing a background check on Mr. Donovan. He's a suspect in some other crimes."

"More thefts and bullying?"

"Of a sort," I said. "Let's just say his behavior has warranted my attention."

Outside the windows, the day campers were dipping gallon buckets into the marsh and sorting through the muck. Some of the children carried long nets. They wore rubber boots and sloshed about, seeming to have a great time. All in all, I would have invested in sailing at Martha's Vineyard. You could have cocktails while the kids frolicked.

"My relationship with Mr. Donovan remained icy," Schultze said. "We didn't speak for almost a year. He did his job. And then he had an altercation with one of our tenth-graders. He accused a boy of breaking into the maintenance shed and took matters into his own hands."

"What did he do?"

"He pushed the boy and slapped him hard across the face," Schultze said. Schultze's own face colored a bit as he spoke. "We fired him immediately. The parents, rightly so, were horrified. As were we."

"How'd Donovan take being fired?"

"Not well," Schultze said. He rocked back in his padded leather chair and folded his hands across his belly. "He blamed several young boys of plotting against him, even saying they'd been the ones who'd stolen the electronics. He threatened to sue the school when the parents of the boy filed charges. And he threatened me with violence. We had to have the police escort him from campus."

"What exactly did he say to you?"

"He claimed I'd ruined his name," Schultze said. He removed the stylish eyeglasses. He blew a warm breath on a lens and cleaned it with a tissue. "And that he wished to kick the crap out of me."

"Subtle."

"He's a sick man," Schultze said. "There's an aura of meanness about him. He wouldn't speak to you or look you in the eye. The only time I ever saw him animated was when he'd talk to some of the instructors about firefighting. He claimed to have been a volunteer firefighter."

"Which is not true."

"He said a lot of things that turned out not to be true."

"What else?"

"He said he was a decorated Marine."

"Did he have a military record?"

"None," he said. "Were you in the service, Mr. Spenser?"

"Army," I said. "For a few years."

"I was in the Air Force," he said. "You and I probably have similar feelings about those who lie about their service."

I nodded. I didn't do much in the Army, but I wasn't overly fond of liars of any type.

"His stories on firefighting and his time in the Marines were very detailed," Schultze said. "He put a lot of thought into his imaginary life as a hero of some sort."

"So what ever happened to the assault charges against our Walter Mitty?"

Schultze leaned his elbows on his desk. I heard buckets being tossed back into the marsh, lots of laughing, and more sloshing. The muck bubbled up and turned the surface water a deep brown. A sign above his desk said GIFTED MINDS NEED CREATIVE INSTRUCTION. The school was brick and stately, with numerous state and national awards displayed in the halls.

I bet a free pony probably came with the price of tuition.

He threw up his hands and shook his head. "The boy's family decided not to press charges," he said. "I was very disappointed. But our board of directors were privately pleased. If this had made the news, we would have lost so many students. We are much, much better about our new hiring process."

"Any idea why they dropped the charges?"

"The family has had some personal hardships," Schultze said. "There was a terrible fire at their home. They lost everything and they had to move. I believe they let go of the case because of all the pressure."

"Aha," I said.

"You don't think—"

"I'm not a fan of coincidence," I said. "Where did the family live?"

T he thing about bad guys," I said, "is that sooner or later they'll tell you the truth."

I was behind the wheel of my Explorer in Southie that afternoon, riffing my years of wisdom like John Coltrane on playing sax, Y. A. Tittle on throwing touchdowns, or Carmen Miranda doing the samba. Z leaned back in the passenger seat, his eyes slightly closed, but I was pretty sure he was still awake.

"Get them talking," he said, "and they can't shut up."

"Unless they're shooting at you. If they're shooting, you should delay the conversation until later."

"A medicine man told me the same thing," Z said. "But he was speaking of the white man. Not hoods."

"You can always call me," I said. "When you need advice. Or the medicine man. Whichever one of us is relevant."

"Or ask your buddies in L.A."

"Chollo and I would offer very different guidance," I said. "But Bobby Horse? He and I might share the same opinion."

Johnny Donovan kept his security office in a one-story brick building in a weedy lot behind a chain-link fence. I figured he didn't want anyone stealing the weeds or junked old fire trucks haphazardly parked. We had parked along D Street, not far off Old Colony.

"We don't want to confront him," Z said.

"No," I said. "Not yet."

"But you want him to know that we're tailing him," Z said. "That we're interested."

"Let's just see where he leads us," I said. "We have little else going for us."

"So, what do we know about this guy?"

"Donovan appears to be a true lunatic," I said. "He's been arrested three times for impersonating cops. He lost a job three years ago as a maintenance guy at a rich private school. He was accused of stealing electronics and later of slapping a young boy. The case was *nol-prossed*."

"Lovely."

"In the middle of the court case, the victim's house burned," I said. "I found that to be a strange coincidence."

"Almost eerie." Z raised up in the passenger seat. We both watched a bright red Chevy Blazer stop at the chain-link gate. A thick guy in a blue Pats jersey with number 87 crawled out from behind the wheel. He unlocked the gate and yelled at a brindle pit bull that jumped up on his short pant legs. He was small, thick, and beady-eyed. He looked very much like a troll from a Grimm's tale.

"At least the dog seems friendly," Z said.

"When the time comes, you might need to jump that fence to investigate."

"I don't do dogs," he said. "Especially pit bulls."

"Hawk doesn't care for dogs, either," I said. "Except Pearl. He and Pearl have become great friends. Sometimes I believe she might leave me for him. If the occasion came up."

Johnny Donovan drove up into the lot, parked, and wandered up a wheelchair ramp to the front door. Despite the windows being down in the Explorer, the interior was hot and stuffy. There was little wind in South Boston that afternoon.

"If Teehan tipped him, he's going to be vigilant," Z said. "Tough to tail."

"We take turns," I said. "Always bring coffee. That's the key to a successful stakeout."

"What about Hawk?"

"Hawk has other duties."

"Making sure Jackie DeMarco doesn't kill you while you sleuth?"

"Yep," I said. "Being dead might hamper our investigation."

Johnny Donovan abruptly walked out of the metal shed of an office and locked the door. The Pats jersey was too big for him but not big enough to hide a large bulge on his right hip. He now had on a ball cap with a red FD logo and a pair of sunglasses. He had a sagging stomach, short legs, and a large hooked nose.

"What do you think he's packing?" Z said.

"From here, looks like a Mauser," I said. "Anti-tank."

"Doesn't deserve to wear the Gronk."

"Nope," I said. "Better suited for Hernandez."

Loose trash littered his yard: fast-food wrappers, foam cups, and plastic bags. A big billboard loomed over his tiny building. A young kid huddled in a corner of the image, under TAKE A STAND AGAINST BULLYING in big white letters. Donovan drove back to the gate, unlocked it, continued through it, and locked it behind him. The pit bull ran nervously up and down the length of the fence as he drove away and passed us on the way out. The dog emitted several high-pitched barks. Running and barking with nervous energy.

"I say we grab him."

"Not yet."

"He's soft," Z said. "Moves slow. Out of shape, with little legs and a big stomach."

"Man like that knows he's beat," I said. "He's a bully. He'll shoot before you get close. Nothing to lose if he's cornered."

"Never mess with an Indian and his *kemosabe*."

"Are you ever going to give up on the Lone Ranger thing?"

"When something works, stick with it," Z said.

I waited a few seconds and followed him out to Old Colony, where he headed north until the road merged with Dot Ave. "Hi ho, Silver?" I said.

Z nodded in appreciation.

For the next few hours, Johnny Donovan zipped around Boston, checking and installing security systems. At a particularly tense moment, he filled up the Chevy's tank and took a leak at a Citgo before walking across the street to McDonald's. Z stayed on him while I met Teddy Cahill and Jack McGee at Joe Moakley Park for an update.

From the park bench, there was a great view of the city from Southie. Several Little Leaguers battled it out on the ball fields while joggers ran past us, stout of heart and shiny with sweat. The late-afternoon light shimmered off the mirrored windows downtown. I could tell by his stoic look under the big white mustache that Cahill was glad to see me.

I'd already shown McGee the photos. He stood with a lot of nervous energy while Cahill sat and patted Galway's head. The old dog's tongue lolled from the corner of her mouth, panting in the summer heat. I pulled the blow-ups from the folder. "Know these guys?"

"Sure," he said. Cahill looked up to McGee. "I seen one of 'em around."

"Have you checked them out?" I said.

"Like I said, whattya got?"

"They were seen at almost all of the suspicious fires."

"It's them," McGee said. "It's fucking them. Right there all the time. I want their asses for all they've done."

Cahill looked to McGee and shot him a hard look. "Yeah," Cahill said. "But they're Sparks. It's what they do. That's like saying you saw cheerleaders at Gillette."

"Cheerleaders don't try and kill the players," McGee said.

Cahill held up a hand to try to quiet McGee. McGee's face was red hot.

"They are not Sparks," I said. "Sparks are good guys who regard this crew as grade-A wackos. Persona non grata at their clubhouse. One of them had a big beef against Rob Featherstone."

"Okay," Cahill said. "I'm listening."

"Listening?" McGee said. "Holy Christ. He's listening. Spenser got you the first hot lead on this thing and you're fucking listening."

"Shut up, Jack," Cahill said.

"Shut up?" McGee said. He walked up too close to Cahill, breathing hard in and out of his nose. I stood and put a light hand on McGee's shoulder. He looked to me and then back to Cahill.

He then shook his head and walked off down a path.

ACE ATKINS

"You can see why Jack's been a pain in my ass over the last year?" Cahill said.

"He means well."

We watched him follow a path back to where he'd parked. I hoped he'd wait in the car. I'd ridden with him down to the park.

"I pulled some video from a local TV station," I said. "After a couple days, I detected some patterns and strange behavior."

"How strange?"

"One of these guys pulled a pistol out like he was going to fire it in the air," I said. "Another one of them, the one with the Shaggy goatee, took a bunch of selfies with the fires. It was like they were all watching a rock concert."

"Names?"

"Young guy is Kevin Teehan," I said. "High school dropout, works at the Home Depot in Somerville, and is a part-timer with the fire department in Blackburn. He claims he put in an application with you guys but won't make the cut because he's neither black nor a woman."

"That's bullshit," Cahill said.

"Yep," I said. "He also told me he'd never heard of a guy named Johnny Donovan."

"Who the fuck is Johnny Donovan?"

I flipped through the pages of the screen grabs. I selected the one I wanted and showed him the still. "The guy he's got an arm around in this pic. Unless he's just overly friendly, they appear to be good pals."

"Still doesn't mean dick."

"What else do we have?"

216

"Dick," he said.

"Two years ago, Donovan was accused of stealing electronics from a tony private school in Watertown," I said. "They couldn't prove anything. But later, he slapped a kid across the face and was charged with assault. Before any of this went to court, the victim's home burned and all charges were dropped."

"Okay," he said. "Keep going."

I handed him a file on Johnny Donovan. I asked him to pull the fire records from Watertown. I showed him several photos of the three having a grand time at different arsons. "I don't know the identity of the third man in the picture."

Cahill studied the pic and shook his head. Two women in sports bras and running shorts jogged briskly past us. Our train of thought was momentarily interrupted. Even Galway lifted her old head to stare. "Maybe it's Orson Welles."

"Donovan's been arrested for some other stuff," I said. "He was charged three times in Western Mass for impersonating a cop."

"What a second," Cahill said. "Wait a second. What's this bastard's name again?"

"Donovan," I said. "Johnny Donovan. Jack said he had some trouble with him before. He banned him from the firehouse. He once yelled at Jack at a fire for not following procedure."

Cahill nodded, thinking on it, remembering a grain of something. He took the leash off Galway and let her trot around in the open grass. Galway took a leak beside a small tree and walked into the wide-open space of the park, sniffing the summer air.

"So you got a wannabe and a nutso," he said. "What's in it for them? Usually guys like that rush in fast and try to save the day. Be heroes. They didn't. Why set the fires?"

I shrugged. "That's where it gets murky," I said. "Motive."

"Any witnesses to put them at the scenes before the fires?" he said. "Did you find them with any of the equipment used in making these devices?"

"These guys aren't MIT students," I said. "They'll trip up."

"Are you watching them?" Cahill said.

I nodded. "Given our situation, Jack and I thought we might join forces."

Galway trotted back from her journey. She panted and lay down on the grass by the park bench. The Little League game sounded in the distance. It was a warm, sunny afternoon filled with possibilities.

"Let me have the pictures," Cahill said. "I can get our guys to go back to some witnesses."

"Maybe I could dig around at Donovan's place," I said.

"Just don't screw it up," Cahill said. "If these bastards are our guys, we got to get it on the level. A good clean search with a warrant."

I nodded. Cahill sighed and reached down to rub Galway's ears.

"You know, I thought I really had something yesterday. A security camera not far from the second fire the night your apartment burned. That bigger fire, down in the South End, that sent some of our boys to the hospital."

"What happened?"

"Property owner won't give it up."

"Why not?"

"Don't know," he said. "I mean, it's a freakin' flower shop in the South End. What are we gonna do, steal ideas for anniversary arrangements?"

"Can't you force them?"

"It's private property," he said. "I tried to talk straight to one of the gentlemen who runs it. He claims the camera is busted. I asked for anything the camera had anyway, and he tells me to contact his lawyer. Next thing I know, I get a call from an attorney talking about harassment. I mean, what the hell?"

With great effort, Galway got to her feet and snuffled over to me. She sniffed at my pant leg and her tail began to wag. I figured she'd caught scent of Miss Pearl.

"Maybe I can help."

"Are you talking about something illegal or unethical?"

I smiled. "Goodness, no."

We can leave it all alone," Johnny Donovan said. "Or we can double the fuck down and do the job we agreed to do."

Big Ray reached for a donut and took a huge bite in an effort to stay silent. Johnny watched him for a moment and then turned to Kevin. Kevin took a cool sip of water and waited. He knew Johnny was cracking a bit. He just hoped he'd hold it together in case someone saw them gathered at the Scandinavian Pastry shop.

"This is it," Johnny said. "Draw the fucking line. Teach those bastards a lesson. This is the twenty-first century. You can't run a department with no freakin' money. Old equipment and jalopy trucks. Action. We need action."

"That guy you told me about," Kevin said. He didn't want to tell but had to tell him. "The investigator? He came to me at work. He started asking me what I'd seen at these fires. Asked me a lot about the church in the South End. And he asked me if you and I were friends."

"Son of a bitch."

Big Ray stopped chewing. He just cut his eyes from left to right where Kevin and Johnny sat side by side. He was dressed in civilian clothes tonight. They had plans for a couple places in Brighton just to expand their territory, let the department know that no neighborhood was safe.

"What did he know?" Ray said.

"I don't think he knew nothing," Kevin said. "I think he was just fishing around. Someone told him we'd been sparking and he thought he'd run some questions by me. I don't know. I didn't think much of it until he got serious about Johnny. He seemed like he wanted to know more about you."

Kevin turned his head to Johnny.

Johnny pounded his fist on the table. "That fucker Featherstone," he said. "That son of a bitch. He liked me for the church. He was always jealous and suspicious. I don't know what this snoop is doing or who's paying him. But this ain't good. Somebody from the department, Cahill or one of his shit heels, will come to you guys soon. They're gonna put on some pressure. But you got to know they don't know shit. Don't get nervous and stupid."

Big Ray nodded. He scratched his nose and looked down at the empty box. "Can I have that last one?"

Johnny gritted his teeth, snatched the box, and crumpled it into a ball. He walked over to the trash bin and tossed it inside. Waddling back to his seat, he shook his head. "We sticking on this?" he said. "We together on all of it?"

Kevin exchanged looks with Big Ray. Neither of them liked what they were seeing in Johnny.

"We lay low for a while," Johnny said. "Somebody is out there watching us. They are waiting for us to fuck up. But we're not going to. We're gonna sit right here and finish our coffee and then go home just like regular Joes. They can chase around all they want, but then they'll get bored and that's when Mr. Firebug returns."

Ray shook his head and let out a breath. "Why the hell'd you do that with my donut?" he said. "Jesus, Johnny."

Johnny tossed a five spot at Ray and told him to get another half-dozen.

S o close," Z said. "Yet so far."

"I'm fairly certain they're mocking us," I said.

Kevin Teehan, Johnny Donovan, and a third man—who may or may not have been the man from the still—sat in a back booth at the Scandinavian Pastry shop off West Broadway. They were drinking coffee and eating donuts. With the windows open, you could smell the donuts.

"Maybe if I run in for a couple," Z said. "No one would notice."

"A six-foot-two, two-hundred-thirty-pound American Indian in Southie?" I said. "Can you tell what they're eating?"

"I hate to say," Z said. He looked through the long lens of my Canon Rebel, clicking away. "It might only lead to tears."

"Need I remind you, I just got torched out of my apartment and lost all my worldly possessions?"

"Chocolate glazed. Maybe a cinnamon or two."

"You're right," I said. "Shouldn't have told me."

Z snapped off a few more shots and placed the camera in the backseat of the Explorer. I took a sip of a bottled water we'd brought from the gym. He crossed his arms over his chest and closed his eyes. When there was action, he was all intensity and energy. But when we waited, he could rest anywhere. I was envious.

"Does it bother you that you will have to start over in L.A.?" I said. "With a new mentor and a more rigorous process to get your license?"

"License," he said. "I don't need a stinking license."

"My introductions on the West Coast are only if you need help," I said. "Not a place of employment. Whatever you do, don't work for Del Rio."

"You said he's an honorable man," he said. "And can be trusted."

"He's also a ruthless criminal."

"I want to do what you do."

I nodded. "And to do that, you have to get licensed."

"And to do what Hawk does?"

"Attitude," I said.

Inside the pastry shop, the merry trio threw their heads back in laughter. Johnny Donovan was laughing so hard he slapped the table a few times. Teehan said something else and pointed to Johnny and then ate half a donut. I waited for Johnny to pull a gun and fire a few rounds into the air like he had in the video.

"I do want to thank you," Z said.

ACE ATKINS

I inhaled a long breath through my nose and held up a hand to dismiss any adulation. Adulation couldn't be appreciated in the absence of donuts. Or good beer.

"I was a mess when I came here."

"You would have found a way," I said. "Tough-minded people always do."

"If you or Hawk ever need me."

I nodded. There was no more to say.

We watched the trio stand behind the plate-glass window. It wasn't unlike watching animals in a zoo display. Donovan walked back toward the bathrooms. Teehan and the third man walked out toward a parking lot shared with an all-night packie. Z reached back for the camera, took a few pics, and handed me the camera. The third man was tall and lean with close-cropped silver hair. He had on khaki cargo shorts and a basic black T-shirt.

He drove off in a black sedan. It looked almost like police issue but I didn't want to entertain any more conspiracy theories on an empty stomach.

"Did you get a shot of the plate?" Z said.

"You may be the one from Montana," I said. "But this ain't my first rodeo."

I waited a full minute and drove away, U-turning south on Dot Ave. I told him what I'd learned from Teddy Cahill, and why Cahill suspected the property owner near the church had been apprehensive about turning over the security camera feed.

"So we might have to persuade them," Z said.

226

"It may be bad karma to pistol-whip a florist."

"Is this considered breaking the law?"

"I'm pretty sure what we're doing isn't legal or ethical."

Z smiled very wide. The idea intrigued him. Watch out, City of Angels.

T his fire that may be on video," Z said. "It started before or
after your apartment?"

"After," I said. "Arson thinks someone played the fire department. They waited until several companies headed to the
Back Bay and then set this warehouse on fire."

"Just to make sure you knew."

"We're two blocks from Holy Innocents," I said. "So it seems
to be another not-so-subtle message."

"How are the firefighters?"

"Still in the hospital," I said. "Burns and some nasty smoke
inhalation."

I drove for a couple blocks off Tremont Street deep in the
South End. On the next pass, we spotted a two-story brick
building set off from the other warehouses. It had a chain-link

fence around the perimeter and a sign reading BOSTON FLO-
RAL. For the next hour or so, we watched several cars and vans
come and go, a gate sliding open and shut behind them. We
noted nothing suspicious. But we did spot at least two video
cameras on the corners of the building.

"Busy for two a.m."

I nodded. "Everyone loves a bouquet."

"If it's a legit operation," Z said, "they'd have no problem
with me stopping in. Asking for a dozen roses."

"True."

"And if not," Z said. "They might take great exception and
get nasty and physical."

"Also true."

"But at least we'd know who we're dealing with," Z said.
"And what to expect."

I started the Explorer and drove close to the gate. We waited
for ten minutes until the gate slid open again and a green van
departed. I darted into the warehouse lot just as the gate closed.
The lot was empty. We got out of the Explorer just as two men
walked out of the warehouse. I was no expert, but they did not
appear to be florists. One man was black and muscular, the
other was white and doughy. They both carried shotguns.

"I'm looking to purchase a pick-me-up bouquet," I said. "Pref-
erably with polka dots and posies."

"We don't sell to the public," said the white guy. "Get the
fuck outta here."

"Don't you guys arrange more than flowers?" Z said.

"They arrange smiles," I said. I kept walking toward the

landing, arms outstretched, showing my palms. Z walked in stride with me. The black man stood still, eyeing us, shotgun held in his left hand.

"How about just one?" I said. "Surely you can just sell me one red rose?"

"I said, get the fuck outta here," the white guy said. "You can't just drive on in a private business like that. Christ, you're gonna get yourself fucking shot."

The black man walked up behind him. He held the gun in both hands now. It was a sawed-off Mossberg with lots of electrical tape on the grip.

"Ma's going to be so disappointed," Z said. His Boston accent was nearly passable.

I smiled, caught Z's eye, and nodded.

Z hit the black man very fast and very hard in the face. He fell backward off the platform and onto the asphalt. The white man tried to raise the shotgun before I punched him in the stomach and took away the gun. It was also a shotgun, a 12-gauge Browning with a walnut stock. Perfect to shoot doves.

The man looked up at me as he tried to catch his breath. I raised his shotgun at him and told him if he moved I'd blow his fucking head off.

Z had the black man by the arm, his pistol at the base of the man's neck. Z held on to the man's shotgun in his right hand.

"Now, about those flowers," I said.

We marched them up to the landing. There was a white metal door with another security camera over it. "Who's inside?"

"Binky."

"Binky?" I said. "Really?"

He nodded. "Yeah," he said. "It's his fucking name."

"Call him what you want. But if there's someone else inside, we'll shoot you both."

He unlocked the door and we walked inside to an open first floor. Several luxury cars and SUVs were parked inside the cavernous space. Long fluorescent lights were strung intermittently overhead, giving off the bright glow of a Super Target.

Another black man stood at a table. He wore a lightweight black leather coat over a white tank top. He had on a blue scally cap and his hands were full of money. On the table were hundreds of small plastic packets, more money, some handguns, and several cell phones.

"Hiya, Binky," I said.

"Motherfucker," he said. It was less of an insult than a moment of realization.

"Hands up," Z said.

I pushed the white guy over by Binky. I explained what would happen if either one of them lowered their hands. Z pushed the guy he'd punched in the face to join his friends. He was bleeding all over himself. Black and white thugs together. Progress.

"Where do you keep your security tapes?" I said.

"Ain't no tapes, old man," the young black man said. "You a cop?"

"Maybe," I said. "Or maybe I'm with FTD. You might very well lose your florist license."

"Go fuck yourself."

Z walked over to the table and flicked through a laptop computer. "Where's the hard drive?"

Binky looked to the muscular black man. The muscular black man shook his head. "No fucking way," he said. "You get us killed, man."

"It's late," I said. "I'm getting tired."

"That's all somewhere else," Binky said. "I don't fuck with any of it. It's all wireless to the server. Anything older than a day feeds there."

"Where and to whom?" I said.

"What does it matter?" Binky said.

"You know that fire two nights ago?"

Binky nodded. He was quick, bright. A real future in management.

"That's why it matters," I said.

Binky shook his head some more. He looked at me under his cute blue hat with dead eyes and shrugged. "Man, you don't know the kind of shit you got yourself into."

"How about we call the cops and let them sort out the details?"

"Suck it," the white guy said. Leave it to the white guy to say something unclever.

"Where'd the video go?" I said.

I reached for my cell phone and started to punch up the cops. I wasn't thrilled about explaining what we were up to, but it might be the only way.

"Okay," Binky said. "Okay. You want that video? You got to see the man."

"And who's the man?" I said.

Binky looked over to his two pals. With hands over their

heads, both of the men nodded. Binky looked at me. "Ever heard the name Jackie DeMarco?"

"Yep," I said. "I'd often wondered why he was shaking down people in this neighborhood. Now I know. It's all part of Jackie-land."

"Goddamn right it is," Binky said. "And you is fucked."

"Well put," I said.

I looked to the money on the table and told Z to scoop it all up with the guns. We exchanged looks. I nodded in appreciation.

"But," I said. "I'd be willing to bet he'd make a trade first."

The money and guns safely stashed, I returned to Susan's at daybreak. I let myself in, let Pearl out, and made myself a poached egg and rye toast. As coffee started to brew, Susan came into the kitchen. I needed a shower and a change of clothes. I had a dash of blood on my T-shirt from our adventure in the South End.

"Poached egg?" I said.

"What time is it?"

"Don't ask."

I filled Pearl's bowl with food and brought Susan a coffee. I added some milk to a small pitcher and brought it over with the sugar dish. She gave me a sleepy smile.

"It was a long if not fruitful night."

I took a seat across from her at the kitchen table with my plate.

"We located an important piece of evidence for Jack Mc-Gee's case."

"That's terrific."

"It would be terrific if it were in my possession," I said. "But it's owned by a man who doesn't like me very much right now."

"Who?"

I told her about Z and me breaking into the drug house in the South End. And I told her about it being connected to Jackie DeMarco.

"Of all the drug houses and all the criminals in Boston," she said.

"Jackie's been a busy man," I said. "He's taken over a lot of territory in a short amount of time. I'd step on his toes with about anything in Charlestown or Southie. But this was special, only a few blocks from Holy Innocents. Now I know why he'd wanted to control that land and any development."

Susan nodded and drank some coffee. It never ceased to amaze how a licensed therapist was open to discuss down-and-dirty criminal activity. Her dark eyes watched me in wonderment, listening to every word. A gold light covered the kitchen table and Susan's hands on her coffee. Her nails were freshly painted a bright red.

Pearl snuffled up and waited for me to scratch her ears. "Am I wasting my time to ask you to tread carefully?" Susan said.

"I am impervious to bullets."

"Did I tell you about one of my clients who believed he was George Reeves?"

"Shall we go down to your couch?"

"Do you think I didn't notice the blood on your shirt?"

"Ketchup," I said. "I should never eat and drive."

"I think it's a terrible idea to seek out a guy like Jackie De-Marco," she said. "Why not just hand it over to your new friend in Arson?"

"Professional pride?"

"Might get you killed," she said. "Just how far has this gone now?"

"Jackie has something I need," I said. "And I have something he wants."

"What does he want?"

"About two hundred thousand dollars and several guns."

"Jesus," she said. "Taken off those men last night?"

I nodded. I tried to appear modest. I had raked in a lot of loot and firepower.

"Did you and Z hurt his people?"

I made a waffling gesture with my right hand. I stood and poured myself a cup of coffee. Freshly ground Sumatran from Whole Foods. I got up for the toast and returned to the table. Pearl followed me back and forth, tail wagging. "Z did provide wonderful support," I said. "I think he's ready."

"We have made great efforts to have a life together while living separately," she said. "But with the fire, we're more connected than we ever have been. I need you whole. Not stealing some thugs' money and guns."

"I collect blondes and bottles, too," I said. The Bogart imitation was flawless.

"Okay," Susan said. "But you'll shower and change clothes before you make me a decadent breakfast."

"Yes, ma'am."

"And most important?"

"Don't get killed," I said.

Y ou are fucking crazy," Vinnie Morris said.

We were walking together through the Common. A guy dressed in a teddy bear costume was playing an electric guitar by the Frog Pond. A group of Japanese tourists were enthralled.

"First you accuse him of torching a church," Vinnie said. "And now you bust into his place of business. He's not like his old man. He's not going to shake hands when it's all over. He'll send one of his people to make you disappear."

"Don't forget Hawk shot a couple of his men last year."

"'Cause he'd buddied up with that judge's friend," Vinnie said. "That shit nearly sent him to jail."

I held up an index finger. "But it didn't," I said. "He walked away."

"No thanks to you," Vinnie said. "Christ. What do you want me to do?"

"Send a message for me," I said.

"Do I look like fucking Western Union?" Vinnie said.

"I don't want this message filtered through his people," I said. "I want this direct to Jackie. I want to meet him alone. I give him the money and he gives me the surveillance footage. He needs to understand any illegal activity will never be turned over to the cops."

"So you're asking him to trust you," Vinnie said. "After you screwed him twice."

"Exactly."

"You got some nerve," Vinnie said. "I'm just trying to do my own thing, keep my head down, and stay out of the action. I don't want trouble with Jackie DeMarco. He keeps to his side of the river and it's copacetic."

"You know he may be a dope-dealing thug and killer," I said. "But I bet deep down he's a people person. Tell him I need the footage from two nights ago. There was a warehouse that caught on fire across the street from his flower business. Some firefighters barely made it out and are still in bad shape. Tell him he can cut out whatever he wants, but I want the footage from the street."

"Oh," he said. "Jackie's gonna hop right up when he hears Spenser needs his help working a case. Maybe you can get him some kind of junior detective badge."

"Why not," I said. "It'll look great on his track suit."

"Hey," Vinnie said. "Don't knock the track suit."

"What's that you got on now?"

"Ralph Lauren," he said. "Pants and shirt. Purple Label. Cole Haan loafers. Alligator belt."

"You could be a mannequin on Newbury Street."

"I ain't making no promises, Spenser."

"Of course."

"And if you turn up dead, I'm not speaking at your wake."

"I prefer you sing," I said. "Perhaps 'Danny Boy'?"

"The fucking lead pipes are calling for your head," he said.

"Public space," I said. "Just him."

"And no Hawk," he said. "Or fucking Zebulon Sixkill. Or any of the damn Village People you hang out with."

"You, sir, are an honorary member."

"Christ," Vinnie said. "I hope not."

We stopped at Charles Street. The fat guy from the bowling alley stood by a black BMW sedan. He had on a loose Hawaiian shirt with palm trees and macaws. But I could still spot the big gun he wore on his right hip.

"Don't call me," he said. "I'll be in touch."

"No problem."

"And I'll let you know where."

"Perhaps Jackie and I could go for an ice-cream cone," I said. "Or ride a bicycle built for two."

"Nothing about this situation is funny, Spenser," Vinnie said. "Those days are long over. Get with the fucking times or they're gonna get with you."

Bright and early the next morning, I waited in the stands of Harvard Stadium. I had on a pair of jeans, a gray T-shirt, and Nikes. I wore a brand-new zip-up Adidas hoodie over my .357. Not that I didn't trust Jackie DeMarco. It just helped me feel slightly more secure.

When he arrived, he was thirty minutes late. And had brought two men, my friends from the Greenway market. Davey Stefanakos and his wild-eyed pal waited at an entrance to the stadium while Jackie walked up to me two steps at a time. Stefanakos looked as if he was prepped to tangle with a matador. His eye was still swollen.

"We were supposed to be alone," I said.

"Oh, yeah," he said. "I forgot. Where's my fucking money?"

"And guns," I said. "I took some nice pieces off your guys."

DeMarco was a little shorter than me, with a barrel-shaped

torso and stubby legs. He had a big head with a lot of black hair and a dominant nose. He wore track pants and a black T-shirt that read DEMARCO TOWING. Probably put his company on his shirts so he could remember one of his legit jobs. Keep his story straight.

"You really want to fuck around?" he said. "Now? I had to feed Davey a sedative before we drove over here. He wants to tear your freakin' head off."

"Might try a chain and choke collar," I said. "It creates a bond between beast and master."

"You ain't getting outta here in once piece," he said. "You know that. This meet. Coming here was dumb."

"But you would have come to me."

"Sure," he said. "Only you seem to got no place to live. You got a lot of enemies, Spenser. Never heard anything like it."

"And a few friends."

I motioned to the opposite side of the stadium where a muscular guy in workout gear stood. I saluted him with my coffee. Z waved back. Hawk was around, too. But one does not see Hawk.

"Doesn't matter."

I shrugged. "We'll see," I said. "We can all fight later. If Davey has a problem with me, I'm happy to settle it. But in the meantime, I wish to appeal to your better nature. If such a thing actually exists."

"If you're talking about me giving up my security tapes, you are seriously fucked in the head," DeMarco said. "I know what kind of arrangement you had with the old man, Fish. You'd stroke him a little under the table and he'd let you do what you want. Or Tony Marcus and all those blacks. But let me deliver some bad news to you. Those fuckers are old. They're as outta date as my dad's Sunday ties. You fucked with me in business that was none of your concern. You fucked with me again about that church fire. And just to top it off, you ambush my guys and take my money. How's it gonna look to people if I don't just shoot you right now?"

"A few witnesses," I said. "And besides, my friends would shoot you first and then shoot your men. It'd be a pretty messy package. And you wouldn't have a chance to march in the Columbus Day Parade this year."

"Eat shit."

"You bring the discs?"

"They're not discs," he said. "It's a whole fucking server. I can't just yank it out and walk around with it. I don't know what you're looking for or where to find it."

"You know about the fire?"

Jackie nodded. As his head bobbed, a thick gold rope chain around his neck bounced up and down.

"Three Boston firefighters got killed by these guys, Jackie," I said. "And this week two more nearly died by your so-called flower shop. Surely you would like to see justice done. These guys are authentic psychos."

"That sucks," he said. "But I don't want to end up in Walpole like my old man. How do you even know my camera caught a fucking thing that night?"

"I don't."

"And I'm supposed to just hand it over and let you sort it out?"

"That's the plan."

I patted two large shopping bags I'd borrowed from Susan. Classics from Filene's Basement. I was surprised how well they supported the weight of the guns. No pride left in newfangled shopping bags. Probably made in China.

"Suck it, Spenser," DeMarco said. He reached over in an attempt to take back his money.

I pushed him hard in the chest. He fell heavy against the concrete steps. His boys came running. Z tried to head them off. Hawk walked out of a tunnel, hoisting a 12-gauge, moving fast and fluid down the steps.

Jackie DeMarco began to laugh as he righted himself on the steps and stood. He shook his head. "Know what?" he said. "I changed my mind. Keep it. Keep the money. Keep the guns. You know why?"

"I'm guessing because I won't live to spend it."

"Goddamn right."

"Too clever, Jackie."

Davey Stefanakos came running up, breathing hard but easy. He had on a white silk T-shirt and gray pants. He gave me a hard, flat look, breathing in and out of his nose. It felt a little like being at a weigh-in. I tried to think of something really offensive to say about his mother.

But before I could, Stefanakos reached behind his back. He stopped in mid-motion.

"Hands up, Zorba," Hawk said. "Or you'll be picking buckshot out your asshole."

Stefanakos showed his skillet-sized hands. As did the other man, who Z had met on the field.

I had yet to move from my seat. It had a terrific view of the field and the stadium. "Sorry about the trade, Jackie," I said. "You know the night I'm looking for. I need an ID."

Jackie shook his head in disappointment. "Your buddies can't be everywhere, Spenser," he said. "Just for the record? You've really fucked up this time."

"So I've heard," I said. "At least I always try and do my best."

49

After my meet and greet with DeMarco, I returned to my office.

I had barely had time to go through my bills when Belson and Captain Glass walked through the door. Belson sat down in a client's chair while Glass glanced around the room. It was her first visit and I noted the admiration in her eyes. I think she appreciated the feng shui arrangement of my desk, couch, client chairs, and filing cabinets. Or perhaps it was the Vermeer prints hanging on the walls.

"I do all the decorating myself," I said. "The file cabinets really set off the rug."

Glass just stared at me. She leaned against the wall and looked to Belson.

"Tag on the sedan that belongs to your third man goes back to the police department in Blackburn," Belson said.

"Terrific," I said. "They love me up there."

"I bet," Belson said. "I made some calls, and it turns out the last one to check out the vehicle was a cop named Ray Zucco. Every heard of Big Ray Zucco?"

"Nope," I said. "Should I have?"

"Quite the whackjob," Belson said. "He's been suspended twice for gross unprofessionalism."

"In Blackburn, I thought that'd earn a promotion."

"He lives out in Brighton but couldn't get on with us," Glass said. "You know where else he applied five years ago?"

"Boston Fire."

"Right you are," Belson said. "Why the hell anyone would want to be a fireman is beyond me."

"Fire*fighter*," Glass said. "They have seventeen women on in Boston now, Frank."

I raised my eyebrows. Belson shrugged and scratched his five-o'clock shadow even through it was only two.

Glass pushed off the wall and placed a hand on her hip. She wore pleated black slacks and a white silk top. She had on a small silver bracelet and a Glock 9 on her hip. Very stylish.

"So tell us what you know," Glass said. "I understand you and Quirk would often share any information. I hope we can continue an amicable relationship."

I put my feet up on my desk. "Amicable means nice, Frank."

He reached into his shirt pocket and pulled out a cigar. He lit up, knowing how much I disliked the smoke. I reached over and opened a window.

"I thought you said he couldn't smoke?" I said. I looked to Glass.

"In the car," she said. "We're in your office."

Belson grinned and puffed out a big batch from his fifty-cent cigar. I reached over and turned on my desk fan.

"Three men," I said. "My associate and I watched film for so long we could've seen a double feature of *Fanny and Alexander*."

Glass looked to Belson. "That's a Swedish movie, Frank. It runs long."

Belson smoked his cigar and ignored us.

"Young guy named Kevin Teehan," I said. "He's a part-timer with the fire department in Blackburn. And an older guy, another fire nut named Johnny Donovan. Donovan is self-employed. He was fired from his last job at a private school for theft and for slapping a kid. The kid's parents filed charges, and a short time later, their house just happened to catch on fire."

"And now we have Big Ray," Glass said.

"The Three Caballeros."

Belson puffed on his cigar and the smoke scattered in the fan on my desk. "Donald Duck," he said. "I seen that one."

I pointed to him with my index finger and dropped my thumb.

"We'll bring in Zucco for an unofficial talk," Glass said. "Maybe just ask him a few questions about Rob Featherstone? Talk to him as one cop to another about Donovan and Teehan. Make these guys a little nervous. I think you're right, Spenser, but it's not enough for a warrant."

"I thought I had something."

"What happened?" Glass said.

"Turns out the owner of that something wasn't a fan of mine."

"Now, that's a shock," Belson said.

I stretched my legs and recrossed them at the ankle. "What about Donovan?" I said.

Belson and Glass exchanged glances. Belson nodded. "We'll bring him, too."

"Any chance you might put that off for a few hours?" I said. "I'd like to speak to Mr. Donovan in person and get a feel for his stellar personality."

Glass thought on it and nodded. "I'm really sorry about your building," she said. "But if you kick the crap out of him, he might grow uncooperative. I wouldn't push him too far."

"Belson can vouch for my occasional subtlety and restraint."

She looked to Belson and Belson reached up and crushed the end of the cigar in a coffee mug on my desk. He flicked off the ash with his thumb and blew out any remnants of smoke. Satisfied it was out, he tucked it back into his pocket.

"You squeeze Donovan and we'll work on Ray Zucco," Belson said. He turned to Glass. "Don't worry. Spenser will do what he says."

"I started to control my impulses just as soon as my knuckles stopped dragging on the ground."

"These are our guys?" Glass said.

I nodded.

"Maybe if we make them nervous, at least they'll stop burning the city," Glass said.

"One would hope," I said.

I caught Johnny Donovan at his office trailer in Southie, where he was polishing his cherry-red Chevy Blazer. I parked outside the meager gates and walked into the lot. He was wearing knee-high rubber boots and holding a dirty rag. Two teenage boys worked on the chrome wheels.

As I got closer, I noticed they were identical twins with blond hair and freckled faces. One of them toted a dirty bucket of suds. They looked up at me but continued to polish the chief's vehicle. Nice to see dedication to such a good man like Johnny.

"Missed a spot, Johnny," I said. "There's bird crap on your windshield."

Donovan just stood there, staring at me. He tossed the dirty rag onto the hood of the car and walked off into a tiny metal building. I looked at the boys. They continued to ignore me and furiously worked on the wheels. Spit and polish.

I followed Donovan into the trailer. He met me halfway, with maybe a foot between us.

"Get the fuck outta here or I'm calling the cops."

"I think that's a grand idea," I said. "Call them."

His eyes flicked up and down. He didn't say anything. I could hear the ragged breathing of a man not in very good shape. His skin was pasty and he had an unpleasant odor about him. Standing toe to toe made his troll-like features even more pronounced.

"My name is Spenser," I said.

"I know who you are," he said. "And what you're trying to do."

"What am I trying to do?"

"You're trying to frame me for burning that church," he said. "You took the word of Featherstone before he killed himself. Guy had mental problems. Maybe you need to take a look at him. What kind of grown man plays with fucking trains like some retard?"

"Hard to shoot yourself in the back of the head," I said. "Twice."

"Huh?"

"And I never said I was asking about the church."

"You went out to bother Kevin Teehan at his place of work," he said. "Featherstone never liked either of us. He couldn't stand that we didn't want to be Sparks. That we knew more than all those freaks combined. We support the firefighters on our own without all that silly club they're into."

"Teehan said he never met you."

"That's bullshit," he said. "He never said that."

"Yeah, I guess he needed help torching my building on Marlborough," I said. "You set the alley while he set the fire by my door. Or was it the other way around? Maybe Zucco drove that white van?"

It was brief. But Donovan couldn't help but grin. "You're crazy," he said. "Get outta my fucking office."

I looked out his small window to the concrete lot. The boys were working to clean off the windshield. They had a squeegee and Donovan's dirty rag working over the glass. Their blond hair stuck up like straw, and they looked as if they'd arrived from Ireland a hundred years ago. The shirts and shorts they wore were threadbare. Their faces were filthy.

"Nice to have good help," I said.

"So whatta you have?" Donovan said. He slipped his hands into the pockets of his cut-off khakis. His V-neck white shirt rode up over his fattened, hairy belly. "Fucking nothing. Show me some evidence if you're so damn good."

"Nah, Mr. Firebug is too smart," I said. "He's a coward and crazy, but pretty smart. I just don't know what's in it for the three amigos. Fame and fortune?"

Something changed in his face. He looked away and scratched the back of his neck. One of the twin boys ran into the office and told Donovan they were finished. Donovan reached into his pants and handed him a few bucks. The boy turned and left. I noted he was wearing a T-shirt that simply read FIRE RESCUE with a shamrock logo but no city and no department.

"You'll never catch him," Donovan said. "You or anyone in Arson. Damn right. This guy is good and he's fucking smart. He'll keep burning this city until he gets the power people to pay attention. If you'd get your head outta your ass, you'll see that we are all trying to help and find him."

"Boston Fire doesn't want your help."

"They don't want anyone's help," he said. He said it with so much force the veins bulged in his neck. "That's their fucking problem. They can't see two feet in front of them. All that smoke has screwed up their vision."

"Aha."

He shook his head. "You're looking at the wrong person," he said. "I'd bleed for those guys."

"I heard they reopened the case in Newton," I said. "That family's home you burned after you slapped a kid? I guess that was a misunderstanding, too."

"You keep on pushing. This is fucking harassment."

"Where are those boys' parents?" I said, nodding outside.

"Those kids work for me," he said. "They needed some money. I do good in this neighborhood. People respect me."

"I hope so, Johnny," I said. "I also hope you trust your friends."

"What the hell does that mean?"

"Two more firefighters got hurt the other night," I said. "Three men dead from the church. Real firefighters can't live with that. They're all family. They'll come find you."

Donovan took a few steps backward. In the small, heated room, his stench was something awful. He spit on the ground and marched to the door, holding it open.

I took the subtle hint and left.

Two days later, as I forced out my twelfth bench press of two hundred and twenty-five pounds, Hawk entered my field of vision. He didn't offer to spot my last rep. He simply loomed over me and said, "Got something for you."

"Can't you see I'm deep into my intense training?"

"Weights will be here," he said. "This won't wait."

I followed Hawk out of the Harbor Health Club. Z was working with a heavy-set woman on a treadmill. Her mouth was working faster than her legs. Helpless, Z watched as we left.

In the parking lot facing the harbor, Hawk popped the trunk of his Jag. He reached inside and pulled back an Army blanket to expose a large black box.

"Merry Christmas," he said.

"It's July."

"This shit can't be returned," he said. "One of a kind."

"Hard to get?" I said.

A couple of seagulls looped around the docks. Pleasure boats bobbed up and down in the morning chop. Hawk closed the trunk and leaned against the Jag. He smiled. The sun was very bright and his teeth gleamed.

"How'd you know where to find it?"

"One of DeMarco's people owes me a favor," he said.

"That's mighty white of you," I said.

Hawk grunted. I could see the edge of his .44 under a light, long canvas jacket. "Jackie gonna be a little mad," he said. "Three folks try to get in my way."

"Stefanakos?"

"Nah, man," Hawk said. "I'm saving his ass for you."

"Looking forward to it."

"We can sell tickets."

"I'll make popcorn."

"Haw."

Deep in the harbor, I spotted the USS *Constitution* making a rare journey out of port. The big white sails full of air, cutting through the mild chop with ease. Cannons boomed off Old Ironsides in some kind of ceremony. Even on shore, I could hear people clapping from the decks.

"Maybe we can borrow that cannon."

"He coming for you and me no matter what," Hawk said. "Things get tight and we just got to draw that line."

I nodded. "Won't the bad guys ever learn?"

The warm sea wind kicked up Hawk's canvas coat, fluttering it off his jeans and boots. He wore black sunglasses and no expression. "You gonna drop with this Quirk?"

"Haven't you heard?"

"Quirk finally retire?"

"Worse," I said. "He got promoted."

Hawk whistled low. "Damn shame."

"And Belson's got a new boss," I said. "Woman named Glass."

Hawk nodded. "Hmm," he said. "She good-looking?"

"When she isn't gritting her teeth. Got any idea what's on this thing?" I said.

"Far as I know, this something you use to play Donkey Kong."

"I'll call Arson," I said. "They have a tech guy named Cappelletti who can figure it out. He's pretty sharp. Although I don't think he likes me much."

"That is sharp."

I'd been working out for nearly an hour. The hot sun and breeze made quick work of drying my sweaty T-shirt. After I switched the box to my trunk, I'd get changed and make some calls.

"Jackie DeMarco's crew will be coming."

"Bring it," Hawk said. "I got no trouble with it."

I smiled. "So now should we return Jackie's money?"

"Don't those firefighters have kids?"

I nodded. Hawk grinned wide.

"Well," he said. "Okay, then."

W here the hell did you get this?" Cappelletti said.

"A little bird brought it."

"We need to know," Cappelletti said. "Sometimes judges and defense attorneys ask questions like that. Evidence can't just wash ashore."

He stood like a banty rooster. He again had his sunglasses worn over his ball-cap visor. As he eyed me, he chomped on some gum.

"Fine," I said. "It was a big bird."

"Jesus," Cappelletti said. He hoisted his thumb my way. "You believe this guy?"

"You know what they say about gift horses," I said.

Captain Cahill and I exchanged glances. He rubbed Galway's head and watched me with deadpan eyes. It had been three days since Hawk had liberated the camera server and I'd handed it over. They'd been going through it hours upon hours ever since. Got to hand it to Arson, they had some true patience.

"I take it you found something of interest?" I said.

"We found a person of interest," Cahill said. "Or what we used to call a suspect."

"Anyone we know?"

Cahill blew out a long breath and threw up his hands. "Your pal Big Ray Zucco," he said. "The cop from Blackburn? Boston Police picked him up this morning for questioning. Belson said the dumb bastard used his own vehicle."

"He's not my pal," I said. "Never met the guy. I was betting on Johnny Donovan."

"Well, it's one of the three dipshits," Cahill said. "We got Zucco walking away from that warehouse only eight minutes before you can see the smoke. This was an hour after your place went up. I gotta hand it to you, Spenser. That flower shop had some primo footage."

"I guess flower theft is a major problem in the South End."

"I don't want to know who or what," Cahill said. "But this is something. This gives us something to work off of. We can push him with this. Let the Feds handle the legal end. We just got to stop the burning."

Cappelletti sat on a desk adjacent from where I leaned against a wall. It had grown dark that morning and started to rain. The day before had broken heat records. The rain fell pleasant and cooling onto Southampton Street, even with Cappelletti's continual gum smacking.

"Any physical evidence at that second fire?" I said.

"Nope," Cahill said. "Burned up clean and neat. These bastards are getting better as they go along. If we didn't have video, we wouldn't have squat."

"Maybe if we knew where you got the server, we could make a fucking arrest," Cappelletti said. "You know that?"

"You don't want to know," I said. "Trust me."

Cahill toasted me with a coffee mug. The rain kept falling. Galway snuffled a bit and resumed snoring.

"He'll break," Cahill said. "Zucco won't try and protect a nut like Donovan. How the hell did a cop fall in with a guy like that?"

"Ever been to Blackburn?" I said.

"Sure," Cahill said.

"Know their cops?"

"A few."

"Then you know the kind of guys they hire," I said.

Cahill did not disagree. Cappelletti scooted off the desk. He started to pace. Cahill and I watched him. Young guys are prone to pace. Old guys sit and figure it all out. After a while, Cahill got tired of it and told him to sit down. "We'll wait to hear back from BPD," he said. "We'll have a long chat with this guy. It takes as long as it takes. But this son of a bitch is going to wear a wire for us."

"How about Teehan?" I said.

"How about him?" Cahill said.

"If he knows you have Zucco," I said. "Maybe he'll talk with me."

"If he knows we have Zucco," Cappelletti said. "He just might jump in the car and keep riding until the road ends. He'll fucking run."

"You ready to bring him in?" I said.

"Depends on what Zucco says."

"You mind if I take a shot?" I said.

"Christ," Cappelletti said. "Do you know how this is going to look to the Feds? No offense, Spenser, but you're going to fuck up the case."

Cahill looked up with his hooded eyes and stroked his drooping gray mustache. "Yes," he said. "But given what he's just turned up, I'm not in a position to disagree. You met Teehan. You really think he'll turn?"

"I think he's a chronic loser," I said. "A true misguided nut. But I also think he's a hero in his own mind. If he sees Zucco is caught, he might just decide to join the team."

"And Donovan?"

"You'll have to catch him with matches in hand," I said. "Or kill him."

"Nuts?"

"Like Mr. Peanut but without the top hat."

"One or all of these guys have killed three men," Cahill said.

"Four, if you count Featherstone."

Cahill nodded. "Let's get to work."

I t was late and raining in Roxbury. Frank Belson met me in the police headquarters parking lot and sat in the passenger side of my Explorer. He reached for the half-finished cigar in his shirt pocket. I held up a hand to stop him.

"Don't even think about it," I said.

"I can't smoke at home with Lisa," he said. "I can't smoke in the car with the new captain. Now I can't smoke with you. Christ."

"It's because we love you, Frank."

"Hah."

"We care about your personal health and want you around a good long while."

"Bullshit," he said. "You hate the smell."

"A wet night and a soggy cigar," I said. "Heaven."

Belson shrugged. He had on the same blue suit but different tie. The new tie looked about two decades old.

"How's Zucco holding up?"

"He did pretty good for the first two hours and then his story started to change," he said. "That's when we showed him the video. And then it all became very real and personal to him."

"Did he lawyer up?"

"Nope," he said. "He admitted to the fire. Me, Glass, and the Arson boys were there."

"And on Featherstone?"

"Nope," he said. "He says he didn't even know Featherstone."

"You believe he's in the dark?"

"I'm not really sure," he said. "He blamed everything else on Johnny Donovan. And he thinks, but can't be sure, that Donovan did the Holy Innocents fire, too. He said Donovan had some issues with a priest there."

"What kind of issues?"

"The kind of issues that got covered up for decades by the archdiocese," Belson said. "He called Donovan a real-life psychopath. He's worried Donovan will try and kill him if he knows he's been pulled in."

"And what else did you guys talk about?"

"What the hell do you think?"

"Will he wear a wire?"

"He's happy about it," Belson said. "He said he's wanted out for a while but was afraid of Donovan. He claims this was going to be the last fire he set."

"Donovan's pretty cocky," I said. "He really flaunted that he couldn't be caught. Of course he was referring to himself as Mr. Firebug."

"Everyone can get caught."

"Justice is always served, Frank?"

"Always," Belson said. "And me and you will ride off on our fucking horse into the sunset."

"Yee haw."

The engine was off, but the windshield wipers continued to slap away the rain. I wanted to find Kevin Teehan, scare the living daylights out of him, and turn him against Donovan, too.

"Captain Glass really doesn't like you," Belson said. "Marty kind of put on an act. But you knew how it really was. Glass ain't kidding."

"She'll come around," I said. "You know how charming I can be."

"I think she's immune to that shit, if you know what I'm saying."

"Even with my dimples?"

"She ain't into your dimples."

"Ah."

"Can I ask you something?"

I nodded.

"How the hell you'd get this damn video?" Belson said. "It's outstanding."

"Jackie DeMarco had an operation close to where these guys burned the church and that warehouse."

"That's why at first you thought it was DeMarco."

"See?" I said. "You can see how I made an honest mistake."

"And you harassed his ass," Belson said. "And he politely turned it over. No harm and no foul."

"Exactly."

Belson shook his head. He reached for the door handle and slightly opened the door. Before he left, he lit the cigar.

"Come on, Frank."

"I'll buy you a fucking bottle of Febreze," he said. "Get over it."

"Wonderful."

He turned to me and smiled. A rare smile for Frank Belson. "You know Cahill told me that someone made a two-hundred-grand donation into the widows-and-orphans fund today."

"No kidding," I said.

"Jackie DeMarco," he said. "A hell of a guy."

The air conditioner in Susan's house was on the fritz, and the upstairs of her old Victorian felt like the lowland reefs of Bora Bora. We lay in her bed on top of the sheets as I told her about my day and she shared what she could share of hers.

"Can I ask you a professional question?" I said.

"Yes," she said. "You are highly oversexed."

"Not the question," I said. "But thank you."

The fan blew an insignificant amount of wind our way. Who knew Cambridge could be so hot? I got up, clicked up the speed on the fan, and got back into bed.

"How do you break up a bond between three people?"

"Now you're getting kinky," Susan said.

"Talking my work," I said. "Not yours."

"Mr. Firebug?"

"Alleged Mr. Firebug."

"I thought you knew."

"Knowing and proving are two very different things."

Susan had on a black T-shirt and a pair of white lace pant-
ies. She turned over on her stomach and kicked her legs back
and forth. Her legs were long, tan, and shapely. How I loved
summer.

"What do you know about the youngest?" she said. "What's
his name? Teagarden?"

"Teehan," I said. "Lost his mother at an early age. High
school dropout. He lives and breathes the Boston Fire Department and all things firefighting. Works a low-paying job but
has aspirations of becoming a true, real-life hero."

"Does he stand a chance of becoming a Boston firefighter?"

"Nope," I said. "Especially not now. But he did apply this
winter. He's a volunteer firefighter in Blackburn while holding
a job at Home Depot. The application I saw showed he is somewhat mentally deficient. No one at Boston Fire took him very
seriously."

"What about the cop?"

"Big Ray Zucco," I said. "I don't know much about him. Belson pulled him in and questioned him. I think he hoped to appeal to a brother officer."

"And part-time arsonist."

"Minor character flaw."

"Who would you say out of the three is the most insecure?"
she said. "The one posing as a hero but knows he's a fraud?"

"In a perfect world," I said. "I would hope all of them."

"But would Teehan, as the youngest, be the most vulnerable?"

"Yes."

"And Donovan?" she said. "You believe he's the leader?"

"I do."

"You want to focus on Teehan's anxiety," Susan said. "If you could get Teehan and Zucco to worry about Johnny Donovan, you might break the triangle. Turn the two weakest members against the strongest."

"That won't work," I said. "Zucco is in too deep with cops now. They have other plans. I just want Teehan to see Johnny Donovan as he really exists. He believes Donovan is a hero and trusts his leadership. Until that breaks, he won't speak with me or with the cops."

"You can push," she said. "But to break the trust, he'll have to see his hero in the act as a failure and someone not to be admired."

"Johnny Donovan has already failed six ways to Sunday."

"Do you think the kid believes he's responsible for the death of those firefighters?" she said. "Or the murder of that Spark?"

"I don't even know if Teehan helped him."

"This sounds all very bound up in a father-son dynamic," Susan said. She flipped onto her back, staring up at the circling fan. "The illusion of the father as a hero is hard to break unless he sees something very real and personal to him."

"How about stone-cold logic?"

"Logic is a waste of time, my friend."

"What's real?"

"Real is experience," she said. "It's visual. Right now, he probably believes everything Johnny Donovan tells him. I'm betting

none of them see what they're doing as wrong. They have justi-
fied all their actions."

"So all I have to do is make sure that Johnny Donovan really
screws up and Teehan sees it?"

"Yep."

"Piece of cake." I kissed her on the cheek. "What do I owe
you, Doc?"

Susan arched her back, stretched, and smiled. "I can think of
one specific thing."

I started to whistle "Heigh Ho" and sang, "'It's off to
work I go.'"

The next morning, the police still couldn't locate Kevin Teehan. I had a few ideas, first stopping off at the Home Depot and then continuing up Route 1 to Saugus and the Riverside Cemetery. I'd found an obit of Teehan's mom on the *Globe* site. An old teacher of Teehan's I'd spoken with told me he'd been prone to sit at her grave. She'd found it a little unsettling.

I parked along a low stone wall on Winter Street for most of the day. I took a few breaks to check in with Susan, eat a chicken pie at Harrow's, and to use the bathroom. I drank Gatorade and watched people come and go to the cemetery on a hot summer afternoon. A man running a Weed Eater and a push lawnmower worked around the headstones. He wore coveralls and protective earphones, and after what seemed liked hours, packed up his gear onto a trailer and drove away in a pickup truck.

As he exited the cemetery, he passed Kevin Teehan in his vintage Crown Vic. *Aha.*

I watched Teehan drive deep in the cemetery, park, and then get out with flowers in hand. He had a mattress and some furniture tied down in the trunk.

I drove into the cemetery and parked next to him with my nose facing Winter Street. I got out, placed a GPS tracker under the open trunk, and walked toward him. He was kneeling at the grave but peered up as I got close.

He got to his feet. He squinted and scowled at me simultaneously.

I help up a hand.

"Police have Ray Zucco," I said.

He didn't say anything. He had on cargo shorts and flip-flops. If I hadn't seen the furniture, I'd think he was going on vacation.

"You headed to the Cape?" I said. "I was just there. Lovely time of year."

"I'm not going nowhere," he said. "You can't just follow me."

"Cops are looking for you."

"You're not a cop," he said. "Just try and stop me."

"It would be my pleasure, Kevin," I said. "But I'd rather just talk."

"This is a special place," he said. "Don't fuck up my special place."

His pasty, pockmarked face flushed bright in the sun. I could not help but notice that there was a scorched piece of earth by the grave. Paging Norman Bates.

"I don't think your mom would like what you've been up to,"

I said. "She supported the firefighters up here. Isn't that right? She was dating one when she died."

"You don't know shit about my mother," he said.

"I know she got sick and died when you were fifteen," I said. "And I know you latched on to a real piece of work in Johnny Donovan when you dropped out of high school. Although you told me that you and Johnny never met."

"I don't know him that good."

"Or that well," I said. "Perhaps you should have continued with your studies. Did you know he was fired from his job at a school for stealing televisions and computers? And that he once slapped a young boy there? Tough guy. When the kid's parents pressed charges, their house burned. The reason the Sparks wouldn't allow him to join was because they found him mentally unstable."

"Johnny's a good guy," he said. "He taught me a lot about being a firefighter and a man. You don't know shit. He's the real deal. He's a friend."

"Yeah, sure," I said. "Ray Zucco says he killed Rob Featherstone and set fire to Holy Innocents as payback for something that happened to him as a kid."

"Bullshit," he said. "Ray never said Johnny burned that church. Because it didn't happen."

"But you three burned other places," I said. "You guys burned about eighty buildings this year. I'm only curious as to your reasons."

"Go screw yourself."

"You guys sent several firefighters to the hospital last week," I said. "You knocked me and dozen or so people out of their

homes on Marlborough Street. I don't like to tie myself to possessions, but I'd rather not lose everything. Do you know how
hard it is to find a black leather trench coat this day and age?"

Teehan looked to me with mild curiosity. He dropped the
flowers near the headstone. His mother's name was Barbara
Ann. She'd been only thirty-six when she died. He noticed me
staring and turned his eyes on me. They were small, beady, and
black.

"What happened?" I said.

Teehan lowered his head and scratched his neck. Now my
hair was as short as his. I hoped the bald look looked better
on me.

"She got real sick," he said. "Fast. Took about a year. It
sucked."

The cemetery was as still and quiet as it should be. Few cars
passed out on Winter Street. Birds zipped past us and crickets
chirped along the stone wall and from behind headstones.
Somewhere far off, a dog continued to howl. I wiped my sweating brow with the tips of my fingers. Patience was key.

"Why'd you guys do it?"

"We didn't do nothing," he said. "Ray is a fucking liar."

"They got you, Kevin," I said. "Cops are looking for you. Nowhere to run to. Nowhere to hide."

"So what," he said. "What are you gonna do? Pull a gun on
me and force me to leave with you."

"Nope," I said. "I'm going to let you run. It'll only make you
look worse at your arraignment. They won't be able to set bail
high enough."

"You and the cops got nothing."

"Everyone is turning," I said. "Johnny's next."

"Johnny won't turn," he said. "Because he didn't do nothing."

"Well," I said. "Whatever happens, I think your hopes of working for Boston Fire aren't looking so good."

"Whatever," he said. "Screw 'em."

"Do some good," I said. "You tell them how Johnny burned that church and killed three of their people. Stand up."

"And make Ma proud of me?" Teehan said. He grinned sarcastically when he said it.

"Exactly."

He shook his head, spit on the ground, and brushed past my shoulder. He slammed his car door behind him and took off so fast out of the cemetery that a kitchen chair fell from the trunk and cracked onto the road. He left it there and sped off.

I watched him go and turned on the tracking app on my telephone.

Someday the human spirit will prevail over technology. But in the meantime, it made my job much easier.

Kevin met Johnny down in the Seaport where the city had dumped a mountain of snow that winter. It was late June, but some of the black snow hadn't melted. They parked their cars on the perimeter of the chain-link by a sign that warned people against dumping shit. But shit had mixed in with the black snow: parts of cars, traffic signs, old bicycles lay in useless heaps like a scrap yard. Kevin looked all around the wide open space and across the harbor and the big warehouses packed close by. Nobody had followed. Seagulls picked scraps out of the mess and flew away.

He got out of the Crown Vic, still loaded down with clothes and his mom's old furniture, and walked up to Johnny's red Blazer with the fire department logo on the door. He tapped on the side window and Johnny opened up.

He had on a baseball cap and sunglasses, listening to the news.

"Where the fuck are you going?" Johnny said.

"As far as I can until the money runs out."

"You run and they'll find you," he said. "There's no way they know what we've been doing. Don't get all squirrely."

"That guy Spenser found me," Kevin said. "He knows you killed Featherstone and set the Holy Innocents fire."

"Bullshit."

"He says cops know it, too," he said. "They're looking for you."

"Ain't it funny," Johnny said. "I just got a call from Big Ray. He wants to meet and talk about things. I wonder how stupid these cops think I am? I said, 'Sure, Big Ray, I'd be happy to meet anytime and anyplace.' You know why? Because they got nothing and I'm not saying jack shit. If they pull you in, kid, you keep your mouth shut. Ray's a nut. He's gotten in trouble with the cops before. Any halfwit attorney could tear him a new asshole. He's a bad cop."

"Where's he want to meet?"

"Where else?" Johnny said. "The fucking pastry shop. But as soon as I get there, me and him are going for a ride and to have a serious talk. I'm going to give him a chance to stick with things, stick with our plan. Boston Fire should be kissing our ass for all we done for them. At the end of the year, the city will be cleaning up those disgraced firehouses, put those old engines out of service. This is a

turning point for all of us. We can't let Ray or some old man fuck it all up."

"Why'd you have to kill that fucking guy?"

Johnny reached for a pack of cigarettes and a Bic lighter on his dash. He lit one up and shook his head. "'Cause he wouldn't shut up."

"What about the church?" Kevin said. "This was supposed to wake up the mayor's office, not kill some firemen."

"Let me tell you something," Johnny said. He pointed the glowing end of the cigarette at Kevin's chest. "Ain't no such thing as a bloodless revolution. If people get hurt, that's because they need better training. Better equipment. When this is all over, I'm going to meet with Commissioner Foley and let him know my findings of the last four years. Somebody in that department needs some goddamn brains."

"Don't hurt Ray," Kevin said. "Okay?"

"I'm not going hurt the moron," Johnny said. "I'm going to give him a chance to go out on top. If they got something on him. Or you and me. This isn't the way it all ends. All this stuff. The stupid Dumpsters and old buildings. It's all been small. The church was something special. The church had meaning. You got to build something that everyone in Boston will see. Like a symbol for people to talk about."

"Somebody must've seen Ray in the South End while we lit up the detective's building," Kevin said. "That's the only thing that makes sense."

"Biggest goddamn fire you ever saw," Johnny said. He

jutted his chin toward a long row of brick warehouses against the harbor. "It'll light up the whole harbor. It's packed with nothing but boxes and wood, old pieces of furniture. I couldn't have rigged it better myself. Probably don't even need nothing more than a kitchen match."

"Ray would never talk about us," Kevin said. "Ray's stand-up."

"Five stories tall," Johnny said. "Longer than two football fields."

"I'd just stay away from Ray," Kevin said. "Don't get near him. Don't get near any cops."

"They're gonna have to invent a new alarm for this one," Johnny said. "Every fucking firefighter and their mother will be there."

"Why'd you start with the church?" Kevin said. "What was that all about?"

"That's where I got educated on how things work," Johnny said. "This is a dirty, fucked-up world. Only way to change things is to write what you want in big capital letters."

W e kicked Ray Zucco loose last night," Belson said. "He was wearing a wire and we were riding close."

"Terrific," I said. "I think. What'd you find out?"

I sat with Frank Belson and Captain Glass in their utilitarian offices at police headquarters. Homicide's offices looked very much like a place where *Time/Life* operators might remain on standby for your important call.

"Next to nothing," Belson said. "He met Johnny Donovan at the Scandinavian Pastry shop in Southie. They sat there for three hours talking about how bad the Pats were going to be this year. According to Donovan, your man Heywood has lost a lot of speed and drive. He says he and Brady have gotten old and need to be traded. He also talked about Boston Fire being an underfunded crap heap. He says that nobody in this city does shit for fire while cops get their balls waxed."

I looked over to Captain Glass. "It's true," Glass said. "My nuts really shine."

"I like her," I said.

Belson shook his head. "He was on to us," he said. "He was playing us and Zucco froze. Zucco lost his cool and started to ramble. He kept on asking questions about Holy Innocents and Featherstone and when Donovan would go off on the Pats or whatever, he'd try and nail him down. Even the guy who makes the donuts could tell he had on a wire."

"Did you pick up Donovan anyway?"

"We were," Belson said. "But Zucco got into Donovan's car and took off like a bat outta hell. We kept up with them all the way to around Braintree and then we lost the son of a bitch."

"Wait," I said. "What happened?"

"It happens," Glass said. "We found Donovan's SUV parked at the T station. He must've switched cars. He was prepped."

I nodded. "Zucco's dead."

"The thought had crossed our minds, Dick Tracy," Belson said. "But we needed a hotshot like you to tell us the odds."

"I'll bet you a dozen from the Scandinavian."

"Spenser, I wouldn't bet a donut hole on Zucco's chances," Belson said. "Christ. Any luck with the kid?"

"We had a heart-to-heart up in Saugus yesterday," I said. "I told him Johnny Donovan was a psychopath and to step up and do the right thing before more firefighters got hurt."

"And how'd that work out for you?" Glass said.

"Oh, he's ready to fold," I said. "He's got good in him. I just know it."

"You realize he's missing, too," Glass said.

"Not necessarily."

"Not necessarily?" Glass said. "If you have anything, you better step up right now yourself or I'll never let you set foot back in this building unless you're being processed."

"Such sweet talk," I said. "How could I refuse?"

Glass gritted her teeth. Cops flitted up and around the maze of cubicles. Phones rang. Computer keys were tapped. I had the sudden urge to purchase a complete set of *The Old West*, starting with the gunfighters.

"The kid has some kind of hero-worship thing with Donovan," I said. "He's drained the Kool-Aid and licked the punch bowl clean."

"And where do we find him?" Glass said. She glowered at me. In the past, Quirk had simply simmered.

I reached into my pocket and placed my cell phone on the table. "Keep your friends close," I said. "And your borderline sociopaths closer. I've been tailing him all morning. He's alone."

"So we wait until he connects with Donovan," Glass said.

I nodded. Belson stood up and reached for his rumpled blue blazer. Glass had leaned back in her chair, legs stretched out in front of her, nodding. "I guess you aren't a total waste to know, Spenser."

"Gee, Captain Glass," I said. "I kinda like you, too."

She picked up the phone and called Arson. Belson and I drove together to reconnect with Kevin Teehan.

They met at midnight at an old warehouse in Charlestown. Johnny was already inside rigging the last few devices as Kevin sat on the hood of his Crown Vic, keeping watch and wondering what his life had become. Thirty minutes earlier, they'd busted the chain-link gate of the condemned toy factory on the Mystic River. Later, in the dark, moonless night, they'd touch off several spots on the second and third floors. To hear Johnny say it, everyone believed Zucco was to blame. And when it was all over, and fires started, no one would come after him or Kevin.

Kevin still couldn't believe Zucco had turned on them. All he knew is that he just wanted everything to be over and didn't want to go to jail. He'd followed Johnny this far, and he'd follow it until things were done. After this *maybe he'd leave Mass for a while, try to find some work at a fire station up in Maine somewhere. Get away from the city, live off the grid.*

"Come on," Johnny said, walking down from the loading platform. "It's time."

The building was old, with busted-out windows and weeds growing through the asphalt. A big realty sign had been staked out in the front parking lot. Along the side of the building, big white letters painted on the brick read TOYS & GAMES.

"Now they'll know it's Zucco," Johnny said. "Let's set this thing off right. I been scoping this place out for months. You'll see it fucking burning all the way to China. It's a statement that Boston Fire needs more men and better facilities. They may hate Mr. Firebug now, but he'll be remembered as a hero in history. We done real good."

Kevin lowered his head and followed Johnny into the building. Johnny shone a flashlight up onto the wooden crossbeams overhead and the stacks and stacks of scrap wood and trash.

The warehouse was dark and hot. Rain water dripped down from the floor above, pinging in puddles. He swallowed, as it was tough to breathe. In a far corner, he spotted what he thought was some kind of mannequin, false and artificial, propped up by a couple of old mattresses and a big stack of tires.

He walked closer. Behind him, Johnny continued to

arrange the tires and douse them all with the kerosene. Johnny whistled "Mr. Heat Miser" from the old kids' Christmas special as he worked. Kevin remembered watching it every year with his mother. She loved it.

"Why does it matter if we use La Bomba?" Kevin said. He walked forward to the big mess of tires.

"'Cause it's his fucking trademark," he said. "The dumb bastard."

Johnny talking now like Mr. Firebug was someone different, a person separate from them doing all of this. As he got close to the pile ready to burn, Kevin stepped forward and looked down into the face of the mannequin—Ray Zucco. Zucco was gray and still, openmouthed and surprised, his head turned in a weird angle as if he were watching the tanker ships sliding by outside on the Mystic.

"Holy shit," Kevin said. "Holy shit. What'd you do, Johnny? What'd you do? Jesus. Jesus Christ."

Johnny looked like a fat little troll in the moonlight, almost like the Heat Miser himself. Lights flashed red and green off the passing cargo ships. He lit a cigarette and craned his head to study Zucco's face a little. "Hmm," Johnny said. "Looks to me like he got caught in his own job. Cops think it's Zucco. Now they'll know it's Zucco. He's dead and they got nothing on us. He ate a gun and burned himself up."

"What did you do?" Kevin said. "Jesus. What the fuck's the matter with you?"

"Good night, Mr. Firebug," Donovan said. He tossed

the lit cigarette into the mess by Zucco and the blue flame started to spread and zip onto the tires and trash. The burn and the heat came on strong and fast. "Now get going upstairs and light it up. We need to get the fuck out of here. Now."

"No," Kevin said. "No fucking way."

"What the hell are you talking about?" Donovan said. "You gone mental? Zucco sold us out."

A little after midnight, Kevin Teehan had ridden up into Charlestown and parked outside an old warehouse by the Tobin Bridge. Belson parked at a safe distance where we watched Teehan meet up with Johnny Donovan. Then they both walked inside and disappeared from view. We waited.

Captain Cahill was on his way. If caught in the act, Belson and Glass would charge them both for Featherstone's murder and the deaths of Pat Dougherty, Jimmy Bonnelli, and Mike Mulligan.

"I'm shocked I don't see Ray Zucco," Belson said. "What are the freakin' chances?"

"They're gonna burn it up."

"And Cahill and his people will have a front-row seat," Belson said. He reached for his radio and called in some patrol officers to watch the side streets in case they ran. "I can't believe we lost Johnny Donovan the other day. He's a tricky little bastard."

Twenty minutes later, Captain Cahill, Glass, and Cappelletti from Arson pulled in behind us. Belson and I got out of the car and explained how long Teehan and Donovan had been inside the old building marked TOYS & GAMES. Prophetic.

"This reminds me of a building I worked when I was a firefighter," Cahill said. "The building was in Southie right off the channel. We had to use the fireboats to attack the other side. They light this thing up and we'll be fighting it for two days. Let's get them before the show starts."

Belson looked to them and said, "Shall we, boys and girls?"

Captain Glass nodded. They all walked ahead toward the gate of the old warehouse. I followed and no one tried to dissuade me. Belson reached for the radio and told the plainclothes officers to move toward the back of the building and watch the exits.

As we got closer to the landing dock, there was a cracking sound and smoke started to pour thick and heavy from broken windows on the second floor. Belson reached for his gun and ran up toward the landing. "Son of a bitch," he said.

A large boom sounded and glass rained down from the windows just as we got under the deck. We heard two sharp cracks of gunfire.

"Holy hell," Cahill said. "Here we go." He reached for his radio and called in the nearest fire company, saying they may need more soon. "We got gunshots. We got fucking shots fired."

Kevin reached for Zucco's body, grabbed him up under the armpits, and began to pull him from the smoldering mess. Johnny yelled at him to stop as he strained and pulled Zucco backward toward the door. The air was thick with smoke, and for a moment Johnny disappeared, Kevin thinking maybe he'd run upstairs to touch off the last few fires.

He pulled Zucco to the landing, where the air choked his lungs as he dragged the body halfway through the second floor. The entire space lit up in bright flame, the heat tremendous and white hot. Kevin coughed and gagged. He wouldn't let Zucco burn up in this shithole. He'd pull him out and let Johnny answer for his killing and for everything he'd done.

He never wanted to be a killer. He'd only wanted to help.

How many now? Three firefighters, Featherstone, and now his own friend. If Donovan wasn't caught, Kevin knew he damn sure would be next. There was a damn good chance that if he didn't hurry, he'd never make it out.

Just as he got to the second-floor landing, Johnny was on him. He punched him in the head and wrestled him to the ground. With his fat little hands around Kevin's neck, he kept on yelling for him to think straight. "Get your mind straight," he said. "Leave him. There's cops outside."

Kevin stopped struggling, and when Johnny's fingers let up the pressure on his neck, gasped for oxygen in the smoky air. He rolled to his knees, the fire cracking and catching in the big old space. He got to his feet and looked through a window at dozens of cop cars with their blue lights flashing. Now he heard the whoop-whoop of the fire engines coming.

Donovan had a gun on him now. "Walk, Kevin," he said. "Leave Big Ray and let's get the hell out of here. Come on."

Kevin's body flooded with adrenaline and his hands shook with fear as he reached for the automatic in Johnny's hands. He tried to snatch it as they fell to the ground, rolling on the puddled floor now boiling with the heat.

He kicked free of Johnny. The gun clattered to the floor.

The men both went for it at the same time, just as the ceiling began to crack and fall in big, fiery pieces.

T his is far as you get, Spenser," Cahill said. He slid into his
fire coat and helmet, with a breathing apparatus in hand.
"You won't see shit up there. You won't be able to breathe."

We stood at the bottom of the first-floor stairwell. Firefighters wearing heavy coats and oxygen tanks brushed past us and
raced up the steps. Cappelletti, Belson, and Glass had gone
around the side of the warehouse, clearing the way for the firefighters and hoses being rushed into the building.

The building swelled and buckled, making nasty cracking
noises, with breaking glass tinkling down onto the parking lot.
I could hear the firefighter's boots thundering upstairs. Sud-
denly the flat hose sprang to life on the landing, a fat yellow
snake bucking all the way to the second floor.

In full gear, Jack McGee ran past me and caught my eye as he
spoke into the radio. He nodded and kept on moving. I stepped

back and let the pros work. I knew the limits of my crime-fighting skills. I may be occasionally impervious to bullets but didn't stand a chance with fire.

Cahill followed the crew.

I walked away from the burning warehouse when I spotted three cops scaling a fire escape on the far side. Belson and Glass waited at ground level, looking as if they were about to follow the uniformed officers. Belson looked to me and said, "We got the crazy bastard on the roof. He says he's gonna jump."

"What are you going to do?"

"Who knows?" Belson shrugged. "It's a free country."

"Which crazy bastard?"

"We're not sure," he said. "A bad guy. Another bad guy is getting barbecued as we speak."

Belson was sucking wind from the climb by the time we reached the roof. Four officers and Glass had leveled their revolvers over a low brick wall, trading shots with Teehan or Donovan. Or both.

Belson and I got down on our hands and knees and made our way over to the officers. Two more shots came from across the top of the building.

The Tobin Bridge stretched out long and tranquil behind the shooter, lighting up the night. Smoke filtered up from both sides of the mammoth brick warehouse. More companies started to arrive, and their sirens whooped and wailed below us. I could hear people shouting and see more hoses being pushed into the building while ladder trucks craned to the higher floors.

The shots stopped.

Belson quickly took a peek around the edge of the wall. He

motioned for the uniformed guys. The shooter was gone. He'd run back down the steps, and back into the burning building.

"You want to follow him?" I said.

"Whatta you, nuts?" Belson said. "Screw him. Come on. Let's get the hell out of here."

Glass nodded in agreement. We headed back to the fire escape well away from the worst of the fire.

Out on the Mystic, the fire boats had shown up and started to hose down and cool the top floors and roof. The dark old warehouse was alive with energy and light. With great speed, we took several escape ladders down to the ground floor. As we walked away from the burning building, firefighters rushed in the opposite direction, toward the flame and the danger. Red, white, and blue lights spun from the fire engines and cop cars.

Belson was out of breath and gagging on the smoke when we reached the lot choked with police and emergency vehicles.

"Maybe this will cure your cigar obsession," Glass said.

"Wanna bet?" he said. He pulled a cigar from his coat and plugged it into his mouth as he walked toward a collection of cop cars.

"Jesus, Frank," Glass said.

"God love him," I said.

"I guess someone has to."

Kevin had shot Johnny. Big Ray was dead, too.

Kevin walked into the flames as the water shot through the broken windows and fell down from the rafters. Firefighters aimed hoses in steady looping arcs, concentrating on the heaviest flames and the roof, where the fire had started to spread. Even after all of it, this was exactly where he wanted to be. He would've given anything to wear that jacket and helmet and be part of a Boston Fire company.

Maybe he could explain to them that he'd been trying to stop Johnny. Let everyone know that he'd been working on the inside to make sure that Zucco and Donovan were stopped before anyone else was hurt. Sure, he'd helped out on a few fires, but that had only been to gain their trust and respect, he'd say. He hadn't known anything about

Holy Innocents. And when those firefighters were hurt on Marlborough, he knew these guys had to be stopped.

Donovan was crazy, not a genius like he'd once thought when he held court back at the pastry shop. That was just talk. It was theory. This was real. Kevin could feel the heat burning his face and hands and smell the hair on his head and his arms starting to curl and smoke. This wasn't like walking into an oven, this was like standing in the middle of a furnace. The coals burning bright and red, even the water raining down on your head was boiling. More than anything, Kevin wanted to be a part of it.

He looked to the firefighters and one of them turned a hose on him, knocking Kevin off his feet and sending the gun scattering. This wasn't the way. He got to his knees but lost sight of them in the smoke. The firefighters returned to his view, his eyes watering and stinging, but then everything was just smoke.

He knew he'd die here. But maybe he'd be a hero when it all came out. They'd know who killed Johnny.

Mr. Firebug was dead. That meant something.

He crawled toward the heat and the flame. A big piece of wood, a crossbeam, dropped from the ceiling and pinned his legs. He heard the crack and knew one was broken. He couldn't move. He couldn't breathe or feel anything, everything black smoke and gagging. He closed his eyes. He would die here. He would just lay down and fucking die.

But then he heard a groan and a pop and his legs still hurt like a bastard but were free. He turned onto his stomach, feeling weighty, strong hands around him. Someone was pulling him out of the bubbling hot water and the deep fire. Before he fell from consciousness, he saw the full, reddened face from behind a mask.

The name on his battered old Boston Fire helmet read J. MCGEE. CAPTAIN. "Come on," the man said. "You dumb son of a bitch."

would have let him die," Z said. "The guy helped kill McGee's friends. He shot at cops. He burned your apartment."

"A few character flaws never deter a true hero."

"Did you ever charge McGee for the case?"

"Nope," I said. "He's helping me find a new place to live."

We were sparring. It would be our last time for a while. Z was leaving Boston for Los Angeles in a week. His three years under my tutelage had flown by. As if to underscore the point, he worked a tricky combination: jab, cross, lead uppercut, and another cross. His cross was always substantial.

"You won't go back to Marlborough Street after they rebuild?"

"Nope," I said. "I understand the tenants' association has a few complaints."

"That's not your fault."

"Maybe not directly," I said. "But after the trial, they'll know who Mr. Firebug was out to get."

We danced around the ring at the Harbor Health Club. Henry leaned against the ropes calling out criticisms and even more complaints. According to Henry, his mother used to hit much harder than both of us put together.

"And how's Teehan's case going?"

"He blames Holy Innocents all on Donovan."

"You believe that crap?"

"I do," I said. "I don't think Teehan has anything to hide anymore. He's broken. He's lost his captain."

"Captain Whacko."

We worked another couple of rounds and then went on to a little heavy bag work. We changed into running shoes to finish it off with some road work. We ran down Atlantic and crossed the old bridge into the Seaport. We weren't far from the Boston Fire Museum where I'd first met Rob Featherstone. There still was a black ribbon on its front door.

"I heard police made a few arrests in Southie," Z said.

"Good for them."

"They must have gotten some good leads off the cameras," he said. "But they still can't get DeMarco."

"Despite his appearance," I said, "Jackie isn't that stupid."

"He's the reason why Hawk has taken a vacation."

"Hawk's handled far worse than DeMarco," I said. "He's working in France. Supporting himself in the lifestyle to which he's become accustomed."

"What's he doing there?"

"I never ask."

Z smiled. "Jackie's gonna come after Hawk. And you."

"I certainly hope so."

We ran past the new Federal Courthouse, where Teehan would have to answer to his arson charges, and deeper into the new Seaport, where the old run-down printing warehouses had become locavore restaurants and boutique hotels. Despite the hip appearance, it still smelled like rotting fish to me.

"I can stay," Z said. "Until this thing with DeMarco blows over."

"Nope," I said. "It's time. This thing with DeMarco has been simmering for a while. It's not going away anytime soon."

"If it does," Z said. "I'll come back."

"I know."

"And you'll come to L.A. if I need you?"

"Why not," I said. "It's been a while since I had margaritas at Lucy's El Adobe."

Z was full of strength, health, and purpose as we graduated from a jog into a run and made our way back over the channel toward the Harbor Health Club. Again, I let him win.

We showered and changed into street clothes, following the steps down to the parking lot. Z looked as if he had something to ask me but didn't quite know how to phrase it.

"Dinner," I said. "We'll have a nice sendoff at Rialto."

When Z packed up and left a week later, it was the only time I'd ever seen Henry Cimoli cry. Just one tear, but for Henry, it was as good as a gusher. When he noticed me staring, he wiped his eyes and said, "Oh, shut the fuck up, Spenser."

60

I t was the first week of September and the first cool evening in a long while. Susan and I walked from the Russell House Tavern, where we'd had a big meal of many small plates, to stroll about Harvard Square. Susan had a vodka gimlet while I invested heavily in a special batch from Ipswich Brewing Company. While we strolled, I noted the trees' many branches and mentioned this fact to Susan.

"Are you drunk, sir?"

"Never," I said. "Simply content."

"Is that your hand on my backside?"

"A pat," I said. "Of love."

I reached out and took her slim hand as we turned on Brattle Street and stopped in for a nightcap at Harvest. She sat at the bar with a glass of white wine, seeming to enjoy each delicate sip, while I had a bourbon with one large cube of ice. We watched the students and teachers mingle and spoke for a while with the bartender.

On the way back, I offered Susan my sport coat, and to my surprise, she accepted it. It had taken some time, but I was slowly rebuilding my wardrobe. A new place might take more effort and thought.

"Have you thought more about us moving in together?" Susan said. "I know there was that one time. But the circumstances have changed a great deal."

"What do you tell your patients?"

"Tell me more about your mother." Susan said it as she imagined Sigmund Freud might have. Her German accent was about as good as my Bogart.

"No," I said. My hand in hers. "Don't screw up a good thing."

"Ah," she said. "You know, I don't think I ever said that."

"Maybe not in so many words," I said. "How about 'Stick to what works'?"

"Better," she said. "And this works for us?"

"Maybe our living apart builds up the animal lust you have for me," I said.

"I thought you said it was primal."

With one hand, I beat my chest like Tarzan. I refrained from the jungle call.

"You can stay as long as you like," she said. "But please pick up your underwear."

"That's how it starts."

She smiled. We kept walking. The crisp air felt good to

breathe, and there was a rowdy excitement about the square of kids returning to Harvard. A sort of rekindled energy from the slow summer months.

"Have you heard from Z?" she said.

"Nope."

"He's very grateful."

I nodded.

"You miss him."

"I had a free trainer for a few years," I said. "He basically retooled the entire gym. But no one misses him as much as Henry."

"Maybe we need to invite Henry to dinner soon."

"He would like that very much."

"And Hawk?"

"Whenever he flies home," I said. "I just got a postcard from Marseille."

"Work?"

"I don't know," I said. "He only mentioned the bouillabaisse."

"Of course," she said. "When he comes home, there will be trouble?"

"I guess we'll soon find out."

We walked toward The Pit, filled with its street painters and drum bucket musicians, the homeless holding out plastic cups. The red line terminal bustled with life, people coming and going into the city. Steam rose from sewer grates while leaves swirled and turned in the brisk wind.

The big digital clock over the Savings Bank clicked off each minute. I looked up at it, closed one eye, and made a gun with my thumb and forefinger.

"Let me guess," Susan said. "You'd kill time if it wouldn't injure eternity?"

"No such luck," I said. I dropped the hammer. Susan and I walked off together into the swirling leaves and music.

ACKNOWLEDGMENTS

My thanks to the Boston Fire Department: Steve MacDonald, public information officer, and Commissioner Joe Finn. A very special thanks to the late Mike Mullane of the Professional Firefighters of Massachusetts. Mike was a great resource and a true pal during the writing of this book. He offered beer and plenty of jokes down at Florian Hall and will be greatly missed. *Boston on Fire*, by Stephanie Schorow, and *Ring of Fire*, an unpublished manuscript by George Hall, were excellent sources on the true arson case that plagued Boston in the 1980s.

Spenser's BOSTON

Charles River

to Susan's home and office,
Linnaean Street, Cambridge

Charles River Dam Bridge

CHARLES STREET

Massachusetts
General Hospital

ESPLANADE

Longfellow Bridge

CAMBRIDGE STREET

ESPLANADE

■ Hatch Shell

State Ho

STORROW DRIVE

State Ho

to State Police,
Boston Post Road

BEACON HILL

BEACON STREET

Boston Common

Spenser's apartment

CHARLES STREET

The Taj Boston
(formerly the Ritz-Carlton)

Public Garden

MARLBOROUGH STREET

BERKELEY STREET

ARLINGTON STREET

■ Swan Boats

COMMONWEALTH AVENUE

Four Seasons Hotel
and Bristol Lounge

BOYLSTON STREET

■ Spenser's office

Boston
Public Library

Copley
Square

Old Boston Police
Headquarters

STUART STREET

TREMONT STREET

■ Grill 23

to Boston Police Headquarters,
Roxbury